RIVERS EDGE

A MACY McVANNEL NOVEL OF SUSPENSE

REBECKA VIGUS

OPEN WINDOW

Livonia, Michigan

RIVERS EDGE

This book is a work of fiction. The characters, incidents, and dialogue are drawn from the author's imagination and are not to be construed as real. Any resemblance to actual events or persons, living or dead, is entirely coincidental.

Published by Open Window
an imprint of BHC Press

Library of Congress Control Number:
2017950864

ISBN-13: 978-1-946848-75-8
ISBN-10: 1-946848-75-1

Visit the publisher at:
www.bhcpress.com

Also available in ebook

ALSO BY REBECKA VIGUS

Macy McVannel Novels
Crossing the Line
Sanctuary

Other Novels
Out of the Flames
Secrets
Target of Vengeance

Non-Fiction
So You Think You Want to Be a Mommy?

Poetry
Only a Start and Beyond

Children's Books
Of Moonbeams and Fairies

Multi-Author Collections
In Creeps the Night

to Mark McIsaac who keeps telling me to write faster…

CHAPTER ONE

etective Sgt. Macy McVannel," I said flashing my shield to the uniformed officer while looking at the door hanging by its hinges. "Where's the victim?"

The officer on duty replied, "No victim."

"Taken to which hospital?"

"No victim, Sergeant."

"What do you mean no victim?" I was getting impatient.

"This was a disturbance call. When we arrived, there was no one here. We cleared the rooms, saw blood, signs of a struggle, called for detectives, and crime scene techs."

"My partner, Detective Tom Maxwell, is coming, help him with the canvass." He nodded.

Standing in the doorway I wondered how it had come to this; detectives on domestic calls. The room reeked of stale cigarettes and cheap perfume. On the night stand by the bed was a lamp with a worn lampshade which had beads glued haphazardly around the bottom. Lying on the nightstand were some tabloids, "True Confessions" was on top. An ashtray full of cigarette butts sat beside the magazines. The sheets on the unmade bed looked and smelled as though they had not been washed in weeks.

Through the worn tacky curtains a neon light from the bar across the street blinked. It added to the dismal atmosphere in the room. The dresser was early junk store and painted black. The top was covered in cosmetics, nail polish, and hair accessories were scattered and broken. The once elegant floral wallpaper was peeling and had faded with age. A red feather boa was draped across the top of a cracked mirror.

I moved to the bathroom, it was worse. The rust stained faucet leaked. The only light in the room came from an uncovered bulb hanging from the ceiling. The shower curtain was pulled back and nylon stockings hung over the shower rod drying. The medicine cabinet was filled with over the counter medications; Aspirin, Tylenol, Motrin, No Doze, Theraflu, Robitussin, and diet pills. From the looks of the dingy, rust colored toilet this place had not been cleaned in months.

Clearly a woman of low status had lived here. The closet held the skimpiest of outfits. Stilettos in a multitude of colors were strewn all over the closet floor. I went through those things with pockets yet, nowhere could I find a purse or other identification. The owner of the clothing, make-up, and nylons had vanished.

According to the responding officers, they had received a 911 call about a fight going on in this room. On arriving they found the door off the hinges. It was one of six rooms on this floor, rented by the week. This one was paid two weeks in advance. It was up to my partner and me to make sense of the scene.

There were obvious signs a scuffle had taken place. My partner would be canvassing the other five rooms on this floor for information. Crime scene techs were dusting for prints, taking photos, and doing what they could. No one expected to find anything of importance in the room.

"Hey, Macy, you need to see this."

I walked to the bathroom door. One of the techs had lifted the top off the toilet tank. There a plastic bag of white powder was taped to the inside of the lid.

"Photograph it, tag it as evidence, and see it gets to the lab for analysis," I replied and turned to go back out of the room. That was it. There was really no crime here, unless you consider low living and tacky clothing a crime.

CHAPTER TWO

R ivers Edge is located on the west bank of the Winding River. The river itself meanders quietly through the town. It is about knee deep at the deepest section. Tourists rent canoes from the local livery to paddle anywhere from five to fifteen miles down the river. The biggest draw is the city park on the banks of the river. The town hosts summer festivals, craft shows, music, and an out-door theater there in the summer months. Fishing is restricted to children under the age of 16. The annual sailboat contest is a big draw for the kids. Otherwise it is a sleepy little town.

As a detective in a small town, you spend as much time working in public relations as you do in actual investigation. Today was not going to be an exception. I came in to find a cold case file on my desk and a message to call an Ida Appleton.

The case file was of one Bobby James Appleton. The date on the file was July 17, 1994. It had been cold for close to sixteen years, so it might be interesting to see what had befallen Bobby James Appleton.

Although this was a cold case I automatically reached for my legal pad and began making notes.

Bobby James Appleton
Born April 1, 1974 at Rivers Edge Hospital
Mother: Ida Elaine (Severn) Appleton

Father: Robert James Appleton Sr.
Single birth
No juvenile record to be found…*check*
Graduated Rivers Edge High School, June, 1992…
verify
Employment or college…*not listed, check*
Reported missing July 20, 1994

Investigator's note: Bobby James was a member of a local branch of the Michigan Militia. He was reported missing after a weekend warriors gathering. Members of the group say that Bobby James had not participated. No leads. No one had seen Bobby James since he left home July 17, 1994.

List of those interviewed
Mr. and Mrs. Appleton
Michael David West
Sally Mae Davis
Joe "Bubba" Waxman…*that's a real name?*

No other names listed and no interviews in the file. *Who were Michael West, Sally Mae Davis and Joe Waxman? How were they connected with Bobby James? What happened to the interviews?*

Coroner's report: Decomposed body identified as Bobby James Appleton brought in August 1, 1994. Bullet hole in skull appears to be at close range and is believed to be cause of death. It appeared the victim was in some type of fight prior to death. Several partial bruises found on body. Knuckles appear to have been used in defense. Cause of death, gunshot to the head, ruled a homicide.

Who was Bobby James fighting with and why? Who pulled the trigger? Where were the interviews? Who was the officer in charge? There were a lot of holes in this file. I wondered if I'd be able to track down all that I needed.

I wondered what made Ida Appleton wait until now to seek more information. I looked at the crime scene photos. First stop I was making would be at the place where the body had been found. I picked up the phone to call Xavier Collins in photography. He took all the photos for us.

"Collins, what you need shot?"

"Funny, Xavier," I chuckled, "It's Macy, I need to know if you remember the Bobby James Appleton case?"

"Sure do. It's been cold for sixteen years."

"Well, it hit my desk this morning. Do you remember where the body was found?"

"Seems to me it was some field, out near Jenkins Corners, let me check my notes."

"Sure, I can wait," I replied thinking he would be able to give me the location.

"So, Macy, when are you going to cave and go to dinner with me?" Xavier asked as he went through his files.

I could hear the papers as he shuffled through the files. "Xavier, you know I never mix business with pleasure and you're strictly business," I teased.

"You're breaking my heart here, Macy," he complained, "Ah, here it is. Yep, Jenkins Corners the field on the northwest corner about a half mile in. Body was under a stand of trees, covered with leaves."

"Thanks, I owe you one," I said.

"You always tell me things to tease, Macy. This time I'm going to hold you to it," he chuckled.

Looks like I get a road trip to Jenkins Corners. It was about 10 miles north of town. There was nothing there anymore. Once there had been a general store and gas station. It belonged to someone named Jenkins who had managed to buy two of the four corners. He had been hoping to start a town there. It never happened. I left a note for my partner, Tom Maxwell, and headed for my car.

Ten minutes later and I was at Jenkins Corner. I found the old general store or what was left of it on the southeast corner. The gas station had stood on the southwest corner, however it had been torn down and there was nothing there but dust. The northeast corner was a farm field; the cornstalks were about half the height they would be before the summer was over. I found a place to park my car and headed into the northwest field. I was not sure what I was hoping to find, but I did want to see where the body had been found.

I hiked the half mile Xavier had told me and sure enough there was a copse of trees. Standing in the shade, I savored the coolness thinking I should have grabbed a cold bottle of water. After a short breather, I glanced around easily finding the location of the body. Someone had placed a small wooden cross there. As I stood there, I tried to imagine what it had looked like sixteen years earlier. I heard a car in the distance. It parked and a door closed. I was so busy with the crime scene photos and trying to picture the scene as it had been, I sensed, rather than heard, the person who entered the stand of trees. I paused in my perusal of the scene, waiting for the person to say something. After a moment I slowly turned. Before me stood a tiny elderly woman, her hair was white; her face was a mask of pain. I believed I was seeing Mrs. Ida Appleton for the first time.

"Are you the new detective assigned to my son's case?" she asked.

"I am Detective Sgt. Macy McVannel," I replied. "How might I help you?"

"My son, Bobby James, has been dead for 16 years and someone on the police force knows who killed him."

"What makes you say so?" My curiosity was piqued.

"They quit looking for anyone after the body was found. Why would they stop unless they knew?" she asked me quite seriously.

I took a breath not sure how to answer her.

She walked quietly to the wooden cross and laid a bouquet of flowers in front of it. "I come here every week and put fresh flowers on this site. It's where he died. Each week the flowers I put here are gone."

"Mrs. Appleton, maybe we should go someplace and talk," I suggested. I really wanted to know how she came to her theory someone in the department knew who killed her son.

"You can follow me to my house, it's just up the road. I have iced tea and lemonade. We can talk there," was her polite response.

"Fine, please lead the way," I told her.

We walked in silence toward the road and our cars. Hers was a mid-sized Buick; mine was a sleek, black Chevy Camaro. Somehow it made me feel ashamed. I followed Mrs. Appleton to her modest home three miles up the road. She waited while I parked my car and joined her at the back door.

We walked in and two steps up from a landing into her small kitchen. "Lemonade or iced tea?" she asked indicating I should sit at the table.

"Iced tea, if it's no trouble," I replied taking a seat. I looked at the small kitchen and took in the homey feel.

She reached for two glasses, put ice in each. She poured iced tea for me and lemonade for herself, then she joined me at the table.

"What do you need to know, Detective McVannel?" she asked quietly.

"You can call me, Macy. I'd like you to tell me everything you can about the week-end Bobby James disappeared. If you don't mind, I'd like to record our conversation. It helps me if I have questions later," I explained.

"That's fine. Bobby was an energetic boy; he became very interested in the local militia. Neither his father nor I approved. His father thought he was wasting his time. He needed to find a real job. He had worked part-time at the local garage, doing oil changes and pumping gas. They argued regularly about Bobby finding a career." She paused for a sip of lemonade then continued, "That weekend Bobby was going to a big camp out. They were supposed to go to some place farther north to the militia camp. He was going with some of his militia friends. He told me he was leaving after work on Friday and he'd be back home Monday morning. I never saw him alive again."

"I'm sorry for your loss." I had questions, but would wait until she was done. We were all aware the militia had camping outings in the area north of here.

"Thank you, my dear. After all this time I still miss him. When he didn't show up on Monday morning, I called the police. They told me he would have to be missing for twenty-four hours before they could do anything. I explained he'd been gone since Friday and he was due home that morning. They told me to call in the afternoon if he still hadn't returned. It was like they didn't even care."

"At the time Bobby went missing, the law did say twenty-four hours. We move much faster now. I don't know if it would have made a difference, but it was the procedure." I wanted her to understand they were not giving her the run around, however from the sound of things they might have been. I needed to check it out with some of the old timers.

"I understand, but I was a mother, whose only child was missing. His father finished his chores and drove to the gas station to see if Bobby James had gone to work first. Bobby James had always been responsible. He'd never missed a day of work. His boss was hopping mad; Bobby James was supposed to open the station that morning, but he never showed up. Finally, his dad got worried. As much as we didn't like the militia idea, we respected his right to make his own choices. Bobby had always been responsible. He'd never missed a day of work."

When she hesitated, I prompted her, "What did you do next?"

"Bob Sr. went to the coffee shop. He chatted with some of his friends and they got together to see if they could find him. They drove to all the places they knew the young kids hung out. They headed north to the campground, but they couldn't get in, because it was locked up tight and there were armed guards at the gate. They claimed Bobby James had not showed up on Friday night."

She was close to tears and paused to catch her breath. She sipped her lemonade and I sipped my iced tea as I waited for her to continue. I put my hand on hers to offer silent comfort.

Finally, she said, "When they got back, my Bob called the police. He told them what he and his friends had learned. If Bobby James hadn't shown up, then he'd been missing since Friday and they needed to start looking for him. It didn't take long before an officer came. He questioned both Bob and I then he left. We didn't hear anything for two days. It was on the news and they did patrol near here more often, then there was nothing. We didn't know what was happening. Bob called, but they were always too busy. When they finally did call, they had nothing to report. Bob and his friends kept looking and we placed posters around town. Bobby's friends came by to see if they could help," she paused again.

"Mrs. Appleton, do you remember a Joe Waxman, Michael David West, or Sally Mae Davis?" I asked.

"Sally Mae was Bobby James' on-again off-again girlfriend. I've not seen her in years. Joe Waxman…is that Bubba?"

"Yes, Joe Waxman is Bubba."

"He was the one Bobby James was going with that weekend. We never saw him again either. As to Mike West, he and Bobby James grew up together. I always thought he was sweet on Sally Mae, but she is gone and he is here every day to help on the farm."

"Is Mike here now?" I questioned. *Talking to him would surely help me to understand what had happened to Bobby James.*

"No, he was here early this morning. He won't be back until tomorrow," she replied.

"Thank you. Is there a chance I could speak to Mr. Appleton about what he remembers?" I asked.

"I'm sorry, dear; my Bob died a year after they found Bobby James. It just broke his heart. He was never the same again."

"I am deeply sorry. Do you remember the name of the officer who came to talk to the two of you?"

"It was Officer Jeff Dunning. Is he still on the police force?" she wanted to know.

"No, he's been retired for several years. I'll try to visit him and see what he remembers. In the meantime, you have been very helpful. I'm going see if I can find Sally Mae and Joe Waxman. Maybe they'll remember something. I'll do my best to see if we can find out who killed your son. Please be patient with me as it will take some time," I told her.

"You have spent more time listening to me than anyone did when he was missing. I thank you for it," she smiled as she said it.

"You're welcome. I need to go back to the station and make some calls. I'll call you as soon as I have anything to share. Thank you for your time and the iced tea," I said.

"I won't call you and bother you. The fact you were willing to listen, tells me you will do your best. I don't expect a miracle. It has been a long time," her quiet demeanor spoke to her loss.

I rose to leave and at the back door she reached for my hands and said, "Bless you for listening."

I walked to my car thinking about what I had heard. *Where were the interviews? Where was Jeff Dunning? Where are Sally Mae and Joe Waxman?* I knew I'd be able to track down Michael West. There were a lot of unanswered questions in this case. I pondered these questions as I drove back to the office.

I pondered a lot of things on the short drive back to town. I have been on the job for ten years. Many still see me as a rookie. I was the first woman in the detective squad of the Rivers Edge Police Department. There are still some who do not see me as an equal but more as an equal opportunity appointment to make sure the quota of women in the department has been filled. Small town police work is still run on the "old boys" network. I am the interloper. It does not matter how many cases I close, I am still a woman, which means proving myself every time I catch a case. Now I have to find Jeff Dunning and figure out if he was a sloppy person when it came to reports or something more sinister. Being the lone woman in the department makes my job very lonely at times. I truly hate the being on the outside looking in feeling. I work hard to be accepted as a police officer but have come to the conclusion I will always be the outside.

CHAPTER THREE

Back at the office I found my partner sipping the swill which passes for coffee and eating a stale doughnut, typical of your police stereotype. Which is where the comparison stopped. Tom was six feet tall and had a trim physic. He worked out at the gym twice a week and coached his son's little league team every spring.

I, on the other, hand stand five feet five inches tall, with light brown hair just below my ears and average looks, don't turn heads…but I'm not ugly. My blue eyes betray my feelings so I work hard to have a poker face. I avoid the junk food always prevalent in the break room.

"Anything new?" I asked pulling out my chair to make myself comfortable.

"Nope, just waiting for you to get back," he replied leaning back in his chair.

"Met Mrs. Appleton and had a talk with her. Do you remember the case?" I asked curiously.

"I had just joined the force, but it was the talk for several months," he replied. "You think there might be something?"

"Mrs. Appleton is under the impression someone on the force knows who committed the murder. She claims they stopped looking for anyone after the body was found," I shared with him. "I find it hard to believe someone would cover up a murder."

"What's in the interviews?" he asked.

"I'd sure like to know. They're missing," I replied watching his face to gauge his reaction.

Tom leaned forward, "No way."

"Yep, the only interview I have is the one I did this morning with her," I stated feeling rather smug.

"Did you take notes?" he asked earnestly.

"No, I asked and was granted permission to tape the conversation," I said.

"Good for you. Make sure you get a backup. We don't want your interview lost, too," he said.

"Done, I did it on the drive in," I smiled.

"Well, aren't you slick? So, what do we do next?" Tom wanted to know.

"I want juvenile, work, and school records on Bobby James. Also, I want them on Sally Mae Davis, Michael David West, and Joseph "Bubba" Waxman. I want to know everything about them from the time they were born to the present," I stated firmly. I was leaving no rock uncovered in this case.

"I'm on it." He picked up the phone and started making calls. There would not be much to do until those reports got in. Besides, it was time to find some lunch before we grabbed another case.

"Tom, bring those reports from last night's 9-1-1 and we'll go over them at lunch," I suggested.

Tom hung up the phone, grabbed the file in question and we headed out. At the front desk we let the secretary know we would be at Dolly's Deli and Bake Shoppe.

We took a booth in the back, ordered sandwiches and coffee, then started going over the report from the 9-1-1 last night.

"What is the deal? Since when they are calling detectives on standard 9-1-1 calls?" I asked, "Was there a shortage on patrol?"

"I think it ties in with your cold case," he replied.

"It doesn't make sense. I didn't have a cold case until this morning. Something is not right here. How does it tie to my case?" I puzzled.

"From what I got talking to the other tenants, the room we were investigating belongs to Sally Mae Davis. She's one of those people you asked me to run. You're right though, they shouldn't have called us for a domestic," he replied.

"Maybe there is something to Mrs. Appleton's claim someone in the department knows who killed her son. Sally Mae Davis was the on-again, off-again, girlfriend of Bobby James Appleton. It will be interesting to see how this pans out," I mused.

Lunch arrived and we spent the next few minutes enjoying the sandwiches. The place was starting to fill up with people looking for a quick bite. With their arrival, we ceased all shoptalk.

Tom told me about his oldest son's little league game last night. He has two boys with a third child on the way. Marriage and children seem to be a great thing for him. I envy him. My life sometimes seems empty in comparison.

I have been so busy proving myself in the department, I have almost no social life. I was an outsider when I came into this position. Which has not made it any easier. People tend to be more suspecting and less forgiving if you are not born here.

Rivers Edge is a rural farm community with a population of about four thousand. It started as a trading stop on the main river. The branch running through the center of town is just a branch. The main river was diverted somewhere north of here. It is the feeder for many small lakes and streams in the area. In some places it helps to irrigate the farm fields. It is a close knit community. There are common names belonging to the town and most of the people here are related somehow. Being an outsider makes you very aware of your surroundings. The first year I was here I had a bulletin board with family lineage on it. I had to be able to keep the families straight so I did not start something.

As a woman police officer I drew lots of suspicion. What on earth was wrong with my childhood I would take up man's work? Why did I want to be in Rivers Edge? Didn't I have my own hometown to go to? Where is my family? How do I expect to find a man, I carry a gun for Heaven's sake? Who wants a woman who doesn't stay at home? Those were many of the questions I had tossed at me when I first moved here. While most of them have simple answers, there are those in town still waiting to say "I told you so."

I've been lucky to have been able to hold my own and rarely have to unholster my weapon. I have answers for all those questions, but I won't dignify people with the answers. It's no business of theirs my father was a police officer killed in the line of duty. Nor is it their business that I chose to come to Rivers Edge after the death of my own fiancé in the line of duty. My mother is in a nursing home so there is no place to call home. My brother is married with four children, so my home is not with him. I wanted to make a home for myself. Rivers Edge seemed like the place to do it, but I do admit, my life is very lonely at times.

Tom tapped my hand, "Come back from wherever your mind has gone. We just got a call."

We quickly paid the bill, walked to the station, and picked up a car. In no time we were on our way to the Appleton farm. This was not going to be good. Patrol cars and ambulances were there when we arrived. The coroner was pulling in behind us. Mrs. Appleton stood on her porch wringing her hands. She smiled weakly when she saw me approach.

"Mrs. Appleton, what seems to be going on this afternoon?" I asked.

"Oh, Officer McVannel, it's just awful. Young Mike was hanging from the barn rafter. I thought my heart would stop when I saw him. I told the police to send an ambulance and you. I'm glad you could come," she said hardly pausing for a breath.

"Have the other officers been in the barn?" I asked.

"I wouldn't let them until you got here. All they did was put up the yellow tape and call for assistance, and then the bus thing showed up," she was adamant about it.

"Those will be the technicians who collect all the evidence. May I go in?" I asked.

"Oh, yes please," she said relieved.

Tom and I walked toward the barn. The patrol officers stepped aside to let us pass. Just as Mrs. Appleton had said, Mike West was hanging from the rafters. There was no sign he had been standing on anything, so this was not a suicide. A plate of food lay on the floor at the entrance. I'd have to check to see if Mrs. Appleton had been bringing him lunch. I was starting to wonder who else would turn up dead and what it all had to do with Bobby James Appleton. Crime scene techs arrived and began the photographs and evidence collection. Tom stayed to talk to the first on-scene guys and I went back to speak to Mrs. Appleton.

She stood on the porch looking lost and forlorn. I sensed she was more fragile than she let on.

"Please come in Detective McVannel," she said somewhat nervously.

We again entered her small kitchen. She went automatically to the cupboard and took down two glasses. Without asking she poured me an iced tea and herself lemonade. Then she sat at the table sipped her drink waiting for me to speak. I took out my tape recorder and she nodded. I pushed record.

"Can you tell me what happened?" I asked.

"I really don't know. I saw Mike's truck here this afternoon when I was fixing myself some lunch. I wondered what had brought him back here again, but decided to make him lunch I did it often you know. Usually I'd invite him into the house, but today I thought I'd take it to him in the barn. I saw him hanging there when I entered, dropped the plate I'd been carrying, and screamed at the same time. Then I rushed back to the house to call the police.

I cannot understand what made him hang himself," she said confused by what had happened.

"Do you remember seeing a ladder or stool in the barn near him?" was my next question.

"No, why do you ask? Oh, no! He didn't hang himself did he?" It was more a statement than a question.

"I cannot say at this time. Will you tell me everything you can about him?" I coaxed trying to take her mind off what she'd seen.

"Mike and my Bobby James met in grade school. They became fast friends. Mike followed Bobby James everywhere. If they were in trouble it was usually because he was helping Bobby James with some hare-brained scheme. They were good boys, went to church every Sunday, hunted, and fished to together. They even played the same sports. Neither was a great athlete but they both tried. They both helped here on the farm. I don't remember much about his father. I know his mother was part of the PTA and on the church board. We used to do things together when the boys were in school. I don't know what she will do now; Mike was helping her with bills and things around her house," she said with great concern.

"Did he live at home?" I asked.

"Oh, no, he had his own place, a little cottage down near the river," she said.

"Thank you, Mrs. Appleton. I have one more question. Do you know any of his friends now?"

"No, he didn't tell me much about his social life. He did talk about his mother once in a while and he asked about me. He wasn't as talkative as when he was a boy," she seemed to think about that for a moment.

"Thank you again. Why don't you remain in the house? Our officers and tech people will clean up what they can. The barn will be off limits for a while. Do you have anyone else who helps with the farm?" again I tried to get her mind on something else.

"I have a gentleman, Mr. Butler, who comes on Saturdays to help out. I can call him and see if he can come by daily," she said.

"Good. Again if you think of anything or need anything, please call me," I said hoping she was reassured.

"I'm glad it's you on the case," she said with confidence.

I nodded and headed for the door. I could see Tom waiting outside for me to join him. We would be comparing notes on the way back to the office and while we typed up preliminary reports, but first we had a notification to make.

CHAPTER FOUR

We drove in silence to the home of Mike West's mom. Notifying families was the hardest part of my job. I never knew how the families would react. This was Mrs. West's only child. He had been helping her out around the house. The house was a small clapboard one. It had been freshly painted and the lawn was well kept.

Tom and I walked to the front door. As I raised my hand to knock, the door opened. The woman at the door was small and frail looking. Her white hair was pulled back in what appeared to be a bun. She was wiping her hands on an old apron.

"May I help you?" she inquired.

"I'm Detective Sgt. Macy McVannel and this is my partner, Detective Tom Maxwell. May we come in Mrs. West? We'd like to talk to you about Mike," I said politely.

She opened the door so that we could enter and asked, "What has my boy done now?"

"Please sit down Mrs. West," Tom said pointing to a well used arm chair.

She sat looking from one of us to the other. "This can't be good."

I took a deep breath before saying, "Mrs. West, Mike was killed this afternoon out at the Appleton farm."

She sat there silently, her eyes filling with tears. She let out a sigh and asked, "How?"

"Someone made it look like a hanging," I replied.

"What do you mean someone made it look like a hanging?" she asked shocked. She used her fingers to put imaginary quotes around "made it look like."

I leaned toward her and put my hand on hers, "Someone wanted the police to think Mike had killed himself."

"He would never do that. Suicide is a sin. He just wouldn't do it." The tears she'd been holding back began to roll down her wrinkled cheeks. She clutched my hand. "Why? Why would someone do this?"

"We don't know yet. Can you tell us about his friends?" I told her.

"He changed after Bobby Appleton died, became more withdrawn. He moved to the little house his grandmother left him and didn't go out much. Sally Mae Davis spent some time with him, but even she stopped coming around. He worked for Mrs. Appleton at first for free then took minimal payment from her. No one would have a reason to kill Mike," she sobbed.

"Mrs. West do you have a key to Mike's house?" I asked.

"I do," she answered.

"Could we get it? We need to see if there is anything in the house which might give us a clue as to who might have done this."

"Yes, I'll get it." She stood slowly and walked toward her kitchen. When she returned she held a key. She handed it to me as if it were some precious jewel.

"Is there someone we can call for you?" Tom asked.

"My sister lives across town. She can be here in a few minutes," she said softly.

Tom stood and reached for his cell phone. "Give me her number and I'll call her. We'll wait with you until she arrives."

She told him the number and sat quietly in her chair. She was lost in thought, consumed by memories of her only child. Her sister arrived in just a few minutes. Tom and I left. It was time to go through Mike West's house.

Tom asked the first question, "Why did someone want Mike West dead now? Wouldn't they have gone after him years ago if they thought he knew something?"

"I'm not sure," I replied. "Makes me wonder what was going on here back then."

"Yeah, I agree," Tom said. "Bobby James dies sixteen years ago and when we start looking into the case, his best friend dies. Something isn't right about this."

"Who are we getting close to?" I asked puzzled. "I really haven't talked to anyone other than Mrs. Appleton and now Mrs. West."

"We need to be careful what we say when discussing this case," was Tom's thoughtful response. "I'm beginning to think there is more to this than a young boy going up against a militia group."

"I'm willing to bet the militia had nothing to do with the death of Bobby James," I answered him. "I think it was someone much closer to home."

The house was on a dead end road. It was very homey. Flowers bloomed in abundance along the walk and in flower beds in front of the porch. It looked as though it had been painted about the same time as his mother's house. The lawn was mowed. It was hard to believe Mike West had kept up two yards along with working two jobs.

We entered a small and neat living room. Off the room to my left was the master bedroom and through it you got to a second bedroom. It was very typical of an old craftsman home. The second bedroom Mike used as a home office, it held a computer and file cabinet. I took the office while Tom searched the living room and kitchen. Nothing seemed out of the ordinary. A coffee cup sat in the sink. There was nothing unusual in the bathroom or bedroom I didn't see anything obvious in his files or on the desk. Tom found a stack of *Field and Stream* most of them looking like they had been well read. In silence we locked the house and walked around the yard. In a storage shed we found garden tools and fishing equipment. We could hear the river at the back of the property and hiked back there. All we found was the spot where Mike spent his time fishing. There were no clues here as to who might have wanted Mike West dead.

We got into the car and headed to the office. It was time to write our reports and ponder why this happened at the same time a cold case had hit my desk. I was pretty sure the two were connected in some way. I got the feeling Tom thought so, too.

CHAPTER FIVE

Back at the office, the records Tom had requested arrived. It was time to assess what we knew. The question was how to proceed.

"Are we setting up a board?" Tom wanted to know.

"Do we have photos of all those connected?" I asked.

"Should be photos in the reports I ran. I even asked for high school photos," he answered.

"Let's set up a board and connect the dots," I replied picking up files and a notebook and heading to an empty conference room.

A board is a cork board where we put the evidence. I'm notorious for making lists; it helps me to connect the dots. It's the part I like the most when working on a case. It makes me think, like putting together a puzzle. I want to be the one who brings closure to the families of the victims, for me this is the best part of solving crimes.

First, on the board was the senior high school picture of Bobby James Appleton; the other was him in death. Seeing his young, fresh face so close to his bludgeoned corpse was alarming. Next to his photo, his demographics were listed and I reviewed them.

According to his file, Bobby James Appleton was born on July 20, 1974. He had died on or about July 18, 1994. He'd been Joe average, playing junior varsity baseball, running, and maintaining B's and C's, with no record of juvenile offenses. As far as I could tell from photos, he had been a blue-eyed, blond with a slim build, which corresponded with the coroner's report, placing him at five feet ten inches and 140 pounds.

He did not go on to college after high school graduation. He worked at a local service station. He pumped gas and did simple tire and oil changes. He was personable and reliable. He had both opened and closed the station for the owner as well as covering so the owner could go on vacation. He had never missed a day of work until the time of his disappearance.

He had fringe associations with a local militia, but had not become a full-fledged member. It is unknown whether this had been the plan for the weekend he disappeared or not. For all intent and purposes he was just an ordinary guy who didn't call attention to himself and met up with the wrong person or persons. His murder was still an open case even though interviews were missing from the file.

Note to self: Find out where Bobby James went when he got out of work. Follow his trail.

The next photos to go up were those of Michael David West. His high school photo showed a young man with dark hair who appeared somewhat shy. His photo in death just reflected an older version of the younger man. He was stocky and stood only about five feet eight inches tall. He was born August 7, 1974. He had no siblings. He had played baseball, run and been an average student, who seemed to have been following in Bobby James Appleton's shadow.

He did not go to college, working doing odd jobs until his friend Bobby James was found dead. Then he went to work on the Appleton farm. He worked there mornings and then at the local hardware store in the afternoon. His attendance at both jobs was exemplary. Neither job paid him a large salary, yet he seemed to have enough to assist his mother and live on his own. His father died when he was in high school after years of drinking, leaving him caretaker for his mom. He was also on the fringe of the militia. His whereabouts the night Bobby James died are in question.

The questions keep piling up. The answers remain elusive. Where were Sally Mae Davis and Joe "Bubba" Waxman? I would keep digging until I had the answers.

> *Note to self: Find out everything I can about Mike and Sally Mae Davis. Were they an item?*

Tom posted the high school photo of Sally Mae Davis, a perky young lady with brown hair and blue eyes. She was born March 13, 1974. According to her demographics she had been a cheerleader, an A/B student, studied cosmetology after high school. She was petite at five feet two inches and 120 pounds. We knew she had dated Bobby James; had she dated Michael West? Her employment record revealed she had worked in several beauty shops and as a waitress at couple of the local dives. We had no attendance record or indication of current employment and whereabouts. Her driver's license picture showed a hardened version of the young girl she had been, with hair dyed blonde and tons of makeup.

She had seen Bobby James at work on the Friday he disappeared, and attended his funeral, but had drifted into obscurity.

I needed to track down Sally Mae. She might be a key to what was going on. She might also hold the answers as to why.

> *Note to self: Was she still seeing Mike West? Did she know where we could find Bubba Waxman? What was her relationship with him? Where was her interview?*

The final photo was of one Joseph "Bubba" Waxman. He was six feet tall with blond hair born April 11, 1972. He'd moved to Rivers Edge after dropping out of high school at sixteen, been arrested for drunk and disorderly, and had a couple of speeding tickets. He was the registered owner of a small caliber handgun and also owned a .22 rifle. He'd drifted from job to job and was suspected of being member of the militia group, trying to recruit of Bobby James and Mike. He had not been seen since Bobby James' disappearance. No recent photo was available.

I issued a BOLO (be on the lookout) for Joseph Waxman with a may be armed notation. He was just wanted for questioning. Hopefully someone would spot him and contact us. I found him to be another key figure in what was going on. Until headway could be made in finding Sally Mae Davis and Joe Waxman, we might find ourselves stalled.

Note to self: Find out what Waxman's life was like before he dropped out of school. Where was he from? Where has he been? Where is his interview?

Tom and I looked at what we knew then we started looking at what we had learned this morning at the Appleton farm.

"You know, someone had to be following Mike. Who would have known he would be at the Appleton farm?" Tom asked, "Why was he a target now? I don't see the connection."

"Someone also staged the scream fest at Sally Mae' last night to get us there," I said. "What was it all about?"

Tom nodded. "What are we missing?" He started pacing and automatically ran his hands through his hair. I could see he was as puzzled as me. "I think we need to pay a visit to Jeff Dunning. It's his interviews that are missing. I'd like to know what he knows."

"Let's gas up the car and go," I said ready for some action.

It was a ten minute drive to Dunning's house. He lived in a modest brick house at the end of a cul de sac. The lawn was well tended. Jeff came to the door in blue jeans and a faded T-shirt when we knocked.

"To what do I owe the honor, Tom?" he asked as he opened the door and motioned us in.

"This is my partner, Sgt. Macy McVannel. We need to ask you about the Bobby James Appleton murder." Tom said without preliminary.

"Well have a seat. Would you like something to drink?" he asked politely.

We both declined. He settled himself into a well worn recliner. Tom and I sat on the sofa.

"Bobby James Appleton, goes back a few years. Just how can I help you?" he pondered.

"The interviews you did, do you have copies?" I asked looking around the room. It was masculine in its furnishings and showed haphazard cleaning. While it had been tastefully furnished at one time, it was showing its age.

"No, they were in the file. Why do you ask?" he wanted to know.

Tom quickly spoke up, "Jeff, do you have your notebook on the case? The interviews have disappeared."

"Disappeared, how'd that happen?" he appeared stunned.

"We don't know. There is nothing but the coroner's report in the file. There is a list of people you interviewed, but no interviews." Tom filed him in.

"Give me a few minutes to go to my office. I might still have the notebook on that one."

He stood and left the room heading down the stairs.

"He seemed genuinely shocked the interviews were missing. So, who would have had a reason to take them?" I asked. The fireplace looked like it was used in the winter, but the books on the shelves next to it probably had not been moved in years. I could see dust on the shelves.

Tom shrugged. "I don't want to go there right now. I want to learn all we can. Then we'll start looking at those who were on the staff when Bobby James was murdered."

"You think someone on the force might know what happened? Could Mrs. Appleton be right?" I was incredulous.

"Let's see what Jeff can tell us first. I'm going to hold my opinions at this time," Tom said in calm voice.

I sat quietly mulling over what Tom had just said. I also thought about Jeff's reaction. Both seemed to make logical sense. What was I missing? Something was nagging at me. I knew if I thought about it long enough it would either make me crazy or I'd figure it out. I heard Jeff lumbering up the stairs.

"Well, here's what I have left," he announced. "I hope it will help you."

Tom stood and took the notebook from Jeff, "Thanks, Buddy, I'll get these back to you as soon as I can."

Dunning nodded, turned to me, and offered his hand, "You feel free to come back if you have any other questions." We shook hands and he showed us out.

"That was interesting," I said on the drive back. "You find anything useful in his notes?" When Tom didn't answer I glanced in his direction. He was deep in thought looking at the pages of the notebook, Dunning had handed him. I chose to be silent for the rest of the ride.

We silently rode the elevator to the third floor. At my desk I started typing up my notes from the Dunning interview. It was an interview after all. Tom was still silent.

Finally he said, "Macy, I think you need to take this home tonight. Read it then put it someplace safe." He handed me Dunning's notebook.

I took the book and nodded. I didn't know what he thought he'd found, but I'd read through it and see what I could find. Meantime I put the notebook in my purse and locked it in my desk drawer. There would be time tonight to look at it.

CHAPTER SIX

I drove home wondering what I would find in the notebook from Jeff Dunning. Home is a small bungalow at the end of a dead end street. I get very little traffic and my neighbors are a kindly, elderly couple, who often take pity on me. I find my lawn mowed or am the recipient of baked goods. My first stop was at the mailbox to see what bills I'd have, then park car in the garage, and in the back door. Once in the kitchen, mail and purse went on the counter and I went to the refrigerator to see what dinner was going to be. Out came some spinach, tomato, celery, green onions, a cucumber, carrot sticks, and cold chicken breast I cut up and put in a salad. I sprinkled it with shredded cheese and Catalina dressing, poured a glass of water and went to the kitchen table. There I opened the mail as I ate. I was delighted to get an invitation to my niece's college graduation and set it aside to RSVP later. The rest of the mail consisted of bills and junk mail quickly dispensed with.

I took my time doing the dishes and putting them away, then grabbed a bottle of water from the fridge and took my purse with Jeff's notebook to the living room. I turned on the TV for background noise and curled up in my favorite chair to read. I also grabbed a notebook and pen in case I had questions. Now I'd find out what Tom had seen which made him think we had something.

I began reading, and didn't stop to make notes, just read it from cover-to-cover, and then I whistled. This was a gold mine. Looking up at the clock I found it had taken me almost an hour to read the notebook. It was time to sit down and see what I really had.

The first interview with Ida Appleton had been an abbreviated version of the one I had taped. She gave the same facts with less detail. It was almost as if Jeff had to drag information from her. Which was out of character with the woman I had talked to. Jeff had also interviewed Bob Sr. It must have been an interesting interview.

Bob Sr. had been an angry man. His only son was missing and no one seemed to be doing anything. His answers were terse and to the point. He had not seen his son since he left for work on Friday. When he didn't return on Monday, he and his friends had gone looking for him. They drove to the militia compound and been turned away. For all he knew they could have been holding his son captive. In between answers to questions he carried on his own diatribe against the police force. Finishing with comments indicating maybe he himself should join the militia.

It gave me a very different picture of the man than what I had gotten from his wife when I talked to her.

Mike West told officers he was to meet Bobby James after work and they were going to spend the weekend with the militia. He was late and thought Bubba and Bobby James left without him. He had been bummed so had gone looking for Sally Mae. Figured he would cry on her shoulder, but he could not find her so he went home. When officers followed up they found Mike to have been at home all weekend. Neighbors had seen him mowing lawn and running errands for his mother. His car had been in the driveway on Friday night.

Sally Mae had had an interesting interview. She flirted with the officers and been vague in her answers. She was out on Friday night clubbing with some girl friends. She did not come home until Saturday. She and Bobby had broken up a week before. She did not like the idea of him joining the militia. He chose them and supposedly she didn't much care anymore. She did play the grieving girlfriend at the funeral, however.

> *Note to self: Locate girlfriends and verify where Sally Mae was.*

The interview with Bubba Waxman was more interesting in what it left out. He could not tell them where he had been that weekend. He had not gone with Bobby James to the militia camp. He decided they were too radical and he was not ready for a revolution. He went out for beers and had not made it home. He picked up some girl in a bar and gone to her place. End of interview.

> *Note to self: See if you can find out what girl, what bar, and if he picked up Sally Mae?*

I had to wonder why there had been no follow-up on either Sally Mae Davis or Bubba Waxman. Did someone know where they had been? This was an interesting turn of events. I had never seen such incomplete interviews. Was Jeff Dunning hiding something? Or had someone else done the interviews? I would ask Tom what he thought in the morning.

The next part of the notebook contained Jeff's follow up after the body was found. It sent chills up my spine.

> Coroner's report: Body found was identified as Bobby James Appleton. He had been beaten about the head and shoulders. He was left for dead, died from a gunshot wound to the head. There were defensive bruises on his forearms. Animals and birds had picked on the remains before it was found. Investigation comes to a halt. Body recovered, the autopsy was done and it became a cold case.

I could not figure out why they would just close a case with no follow up. I wanted to find the person Bobby James had been fighting with. I wanted to know why they were fighting and why they just left him there. They could have called 9-1-1. Bobby James might still be alive. This didn't make sense. This had been a slow and needless death. Maybe Mrs. Appleton was right and someone did know who killed her son and just buried it. Why didn't Dunning pursue this on his own time? I would have.

I *now* had to ask myself what kind of cop Jeff Dunning was despite his reputation. I could not imagine anyone just closing a file this way, especially in a small town. Good cops didn't do that. Why would Dunning? He had seemed like an upstanding guy when I'd met him. I really needed to talk to Tom. He worked with Dunning. He might be able to enlighten me.

I picked up the notebook. Took it to my home office and photocopied every page. I then locked the original in my safe in the file cabinet and put the copies in my floor safe. Most people didn't expect two safes in a house. In the morning before work I would scan it into my computer and put it on two disks. One disk I'd give to Tom. This was something we really needed to work on.

Checked my answering machine for messages I hadn't checked when I came in. There were none, so I took my shower and headed for bed. I wanted a good night's sleep before tackling the problems on this case in the morning.

CHAPTER SEVEN

My alarm went off at 5 a.m. I rolled out and headed for the kitchen. Put the coffee on and went to change into workout clothes. Turned on the TV in my workout room so I could hear the news and began my warm-ups. Fifteen minutes later I began my rotation; ten minutes on the treadmill with arm weights, leg presses on the weight bench, ten minutes on the bicycle, back to the weight bench to lift weights, and finally fifteen minutes of cool down. I was off to the shower and then to make breakfast. I just sliced my grapefruit and was getting ready to use the grapefruit knife when my phone rang.

"McVannel."

"Macy, it's Tom. I need you to get to the office as soon as you can," I could hear the urgency in his voice.

"What's up?" I wanted to know.

"Not on the phone, just get here," he said.

"On my way in less than five minutes," I said as I hung up the phone. I wrapped the grapefruit, put it in the fridge, poured coffee in a to-go mug, and grabbed a breakfast bar. I picked up my gun, badge, and purse on the way out the door, wondering what on earth could be happening Tom couldn't tell me on the phone.

It took me less than five minutes to get to the station. People were milling around. There was a pall in the air. This was not good whatever it was. Tom saw me and motioned me to come with him. He headed for a conference room.

"What's going on?" I asked sensing it was big.

"Macy, Jeff Dunning was murdered in his home last night," he said without emotion.

"No, way," I was stunned.

"Yes, and we are both going to be questioned," he added.

"Why, he was alive and well when we left?" I stated bluntly.

"You know it and I know tt. Did you get a chance to read the notebook?" he asked.

"Yes, it's in a safe place," I assured him.

"Good, don't mention it to anyone. I think there is something very bad going on here," the intensity of his comment got my attention.

"I agree," I said, "and think it's all related."

"Did you have a chance to get breakfast?" he asked.

"Coffee and a breakfast bar on the way in. Tom, I have a lot of questions."

"I do too."

"We are going to have to go off grid to work this aren't we?" I asked knowing his answer before he gave it.

"It looks like it. We sure won't be on the task force looking into the death of Jeff Dunning."

"Okay, we need to figure out where we are going to meet to work on this," I said thinking ahead.

"Not right now. Later we can talk. The captain is calling a meeting soon." He looked at his watch and headed for the main office. I followed.

The room became silent as the captain walked in. This was going to be a briefing and an assigning of a task force. Everyone was waiting to hear what their job would be. Tom and I stood near our desks.

The captain began, "As you all know Jeff Dunning was killed in his home last night. We have a team on the scene. It appears he knew his killer or killers. There was no sign of a break-in. There were two bottles of beer on the end table, both almost empty. Jeff's revolver was kept in his bedroom in the night stand. According to his preliminary autopsy his neck was broken. The bullet to his head, he never saw coming. It was overkill. Those available will be given jobs. Every job is important to solving this case."

Captain Buzz Wellington was an imposing man. He stood six foot six and was as trim as any young officer on the force. He had been the captain for over twenty-five years and was looking forward to retirement. He was also a man who took no dissention on his team. He was fair and took his job as seriously as anyone I knew.

"McVannel, Maxwell, you'll be with me. Sue Drake has all other assignments and will post them in a few minutes. Are there any questions?"

When no one spoke he nodded and walked toward his office. Tom and I followed. When we entered he said, "Close the door and take a seat."

I sat as Tom closed the door. We have to hear what the captain had to say. It did not take long for him to get to the heart of the matter.

"You went to see Dunning yesterday. What was it about?"

"We are working a cold case and wanted to see his notes," Tom answered.

"You couldn't just use the old case file?"

"Papers are missing from the file. I thought we should see Dunning," I replied.

He looked at me, "What was so darned important?"

"The interviews are all missing. I thought maybe Dunning would have copies. I asked Tom to take me to meet him."

"How did the files turn up missing?" his anger was evident in his voice.

"I don't know. I wondered the same thing myself?" I answered.

"Did he have copies?"

Tom leaned forward, "No, Captain, he didn't. He told us what he remembered, which wasn't much. I can't see how this would tie in with his death."

"What's the cold case?"

"Bobby James Appleton."

The captain steepled his hands under his chin when he spoke it was in a hushed tone, "You two find a place to work. I want *that* case closed. To the rest of the team you are off with pay until we find out what happened to Dunning. You are material witnesses believed to be the last people to see him alive."

We both nodded. Tom stood, "We'll take what we need and go out the back."

"You report only to me unless I tell you different."

We exited the office. I went to the conference room, took down our board, and then waited for Tom to join me. We slipped out the back door and made our way to our cars. The first stop would be Tom's to let his wife, Shannon, know what was going on.

The drive to Tom's house took less than five minutes, neither of us said anything. I was stunned by this turn of events. Tom had evidently called ahead because the garage door was open. He pulled in, got out of the truck, and lowered the door. He directed me to the side of the garage where my car was not likely to be seen. I got out and joined him at the back door.

Shannon was in the kitchen, coffee mugs were on the counter. She waited for us to get inside before saying a thing. "So, what kind of trouble did the two of you get into this time?"

"Honey, we are material witnesses in the murder of Jeff Dunning. It seems we were the last known to visit him yesterday."

Shannon smiled and poured coffee. We settled at the kitchen table. It was time to talk strategy.

"We have to continue to work on a cold case as well as the Mike West murder. The problem is we have to stay out of sight."

"Where will you be staying?"

"We don't know yet," he said softly.

"Where ever it is you will be together?" She looked at Tom then at me.

I felt uncomfortable. Being a single female police officer was hard enough. I didn't have the patience to deal with Tom's wife's insecurities. "Shannon, we will be in touch with you daily. We just don't want you and the boys in any danger."

She shrugged. "I know, Macy. I just hate it you have to be out there alone."

"I don't think we're going to tell you where we are. I just don't like the idea someone could try to get the information from you. I also don't want the boys telling their friends. Will you tell them I am doing some undercover work?" Tom asked.

"Sure, they love thinking of you as a spy. Do you need some help getting packed?" She smiled.

"Why not?"

The two of them headed to the bedroom to pack a suitcase for Tom. He also took all the files he had. They went into his laptop bag. Packing took less than ten minutes. We said our good-byes and went to my car. Next stop would be my house.

CHAPTER EIGHT

Pulling up at my house I put the car in the garage. Better to not attract attention. My neighbors speculated on all of my visitors. I let us in. Tom sat at the table as I headed for my room to pack my things, grab the laptop out of my office, the copies of the notebook, and a couple of flash drives. Something told me they would be useful. Within five minutes we were back in the car.

"Macy, stop a block from Hank's Car Rentals. We need something a lot less conspicuous than your Camaro," Tom suggested.

I stopped and Tom got out, then I waited while he walked down the block and rented a car. We all used Hank's from time to time, especially if we needed stake out cars. A few minutes later Tom pulled out in a nondescript Toyota Camry. He headed west out of town. I followed along behind. He was heading for Ida Appleton's farm. I think I knew what he had in mind.

He stopped in the driveway. Mrs. Appleton came out on her porch, as I stepped out of my car.

"Detective McVannel, what can I do for you?" she asked.

"Mrs. Appleton, you remember my partner Tom." Tom offered his hand to her. She took it.

"We have a bit of a problem. Jeff Dunning the officer who handled Bobby James' murder investigation was killed in his home last night. Tom and I were the last ones to see him alive. We need a place to hide out for a while," I explained. This was asking an awful lot of her, but I felt she could be trusted and no one would think to look for us here.

She nodded, "Why don't you come inside and we can talk about it." She turned and led us to her now familiar kitchen. She got out three glasses and turned to Tom, "would you like lemonade or iced tea?"

"I'll take the lemonade, thanks," he said.

She poured the drinks as Tom and I seated ourselves at the table. Once she handed everyone a glass, she too sat down. "Now tell me how I can help."

I explained to her, Tom and I needed a place to stay while we tried to figure out what was going on. "We think all of this is tied to Bobby James' death. Someone is killing anyone who might have known what really happened that night, first Mike and now Jeff. We really need someplace where no one will find us and we can work without being seen."

"The bunkhouse was fixed up for Bobby years ago. Mike sometimes stayed out there if he planned to be here early or do something late at night. It's got cable TV and Mike has some kind of internet hook up out there. It's the lane on the left behind the barn. Wait and I'll get you the key." She left the room and came back a few minutes later with the key.

"Thank you. We'll get settled then go out for food. Please don't let anyone know we're here," I said secretly relieved there would be someplace here for us.

"I won't tell a soul. Do you think it would be okay for me to call on Mike's mother?" she asked.

"I think it would be a good thing. Her sister was with her when we left," I told her.

"Thank you. I'll feel safer knowing you are here," she said. "I was worried because I won't have Mike checking in everyday now. I'm going to miss him dreadfully."

Tom and I left and drove back to the bunkhouse. It was going to be easy to conceal both of the cars. Mine would be first. Then we would use Tom's to get food and supplies.

The key fit in the lock and we let ourselves in. I looked at Tom, the bunkhouse had been used within the past two days. We unholstered our weapons and began a room by room search. The living area and kitchen were clear. Bathroom and bedroom clear. We headed to the other end of the bunkhouse where the three bedrooms and a second bathroom were. The bathroom was clear but had cosmetics on the counter. The bedrooms were clear, but the one across from the bathroom had been recently slept in. A suitcase was on the end of the bed.

I looked at Tom as we put our weapons away. "So, who do you think has been here and do you think they are coming back?"

"From the looks of things lying around it could be a woman. Do you think it could be Sally Mae Davis? Do you think Mike gave her his key? What is she hiding from and where is she?"

At that moment the back door of the bunkhouse opened. We quietly made our way toward the kitchen. We needed to know if this was friend or foe and get some questions answered. Slowly we edged forward so as not to startle whoever had entered.

A young woman stood with her back to us putting groceries into the cupboard humming an off key tune. From behind I could not make an identification Tom and I edged closer. We were able to box her in without her knowing. When she turned around, she screamed.

We stood face to face with Sally Mae Davis. "Who are you? How did you get in? What do you want?" The questions tumbled out of her mouth in rapid succession.

"I am Detective Sgt. Macy McVannel and this is my partner Detective Tom Maxwell. Mrs. Appleton gave us a key. How did you happen to get in?" I gave a firm reply.

"I don't believe you. Mike West gave me his key. He'll be here any minute for dinner. You need to leave," her voice gave away her dislike of the situation.

"Sally Mae, you need to sit down. Mike isn't coming for dinner. He was killed the day before yesterday," I stated without preamble.

She screamed again. Tom caught her as she dropped to the floor. He walked her to a chair and helped her sit down, while I searched the cupboards for a glass. Not finding one right away I opened the refrigerator and pulled out a beer. I popped the top, walked to Sally Mae and handed it to her. Just what we needed was a drama queen, swooning at the least little thing. Wait until she heard everything.

Tom pulled out a tape recorder. "May I tape our conversation?"

"Sure, I guess," she said between sobs.

He turned on the recorder and set it on an end table. Then he quietly began to ask her some questions.

"Where were you on Sunday night?"

"I was at my apartment. It's when Mike showed up. He was really upset. He said we had to get out of town and lie low," she sniffed and took a swig of the beer.

"Why would he want to get out of town?" Tom continued.

"Bubba was back and he knew there was going to be trouble especially with the police looking into Bobby James' death again," she sounded like she was repeating something she had heard.

I looked at her then asked, "You and Mike staged the screaming match in your apartment. Why?"

"He said we had to make it look like I was kidnapped. That way Bubba wouldn't know where to look for us. It was kind of fun," she smiled remembering what they'd done.

"Why do you need to hide from Bubba?" Tom wanted to know.

"It goes back to Bobby James' disappearance. The night Bobby James went missing he was with Bubba. Bubba wanted to show him I was no good for him. They found me at Hank's Bar dancing with Mike. Bobby James came unglued," she told us as she relived the moment.

"We went outside. Bobby James took off in Bubba's truck so, we followed him. We went to the little place in the field. It had been the spot Bobby James and I went to."

She took a big swallow of her beer before going on. "Bobby James was so mad. He was going to stay away from the militia so we could get married. I didn't know. I told him if he joined we were done. All he talked about the entire week was going to the militia camp. I figured he made his choice."

"What happened when you all got there?" Tom prompted.

"Bobby James lit into Mike for messing with his girl. Bubba tried to pull them apart. I was screaming at them to stop. Mike got away from him and walked to his car. Bobby James grabbed me and said something about how if I wanted to be treated like a whore he could do it. He threw me to the ground and we started wrestling. Bubba pulled him off me and started hitting him. Bobby James fought back, but he was no match for Bubba. I went running to Mike. I wanted him to stop it. I climbed into the car. Mike went back but by the time he got there it was over. Bubba had smashed Bobby James' head on a rock. Mike ran back to the car and we took off. Bubba found us later at my place. We talked and agreed that Bobby James was going to the militia camp and we knew nothing else."

"You stuck to the story even when you talked to the police?" Tom was stunned.

"Yes, and Bubba left town the day after the funeral. He showed up at Mike's a week ago. He was messed up and claimed we set the cops on him. I don't know where he's been."

"So, let me understand this," I said, "Bubba knew we were looking into the case again?"

"Yes, it's when Mike came and brought me here."

"How did he know about the case? We didn't even start to look into it until we got the call there'd been a disturbance at your apartment."

"He's got someone on the force who tells him what is going on. I guess Bobby James' mom has been calling trying to get them to reopen it," she said as if we should already know.

Tom looked at me then asked, "So Mike has been hiding you out here?"

"Yes, he said Mrs. Appleton would never know. He was sneaking in at night to make sure I was okay. We were planning to go away, get married and start over."

"When was the last time you saw him?" I asked.

"He was here before he went to work the day before yesterday. He came early. He thought he'd have enough money together by tomorrow so, we could leave. He was coming back tonight. How did he die?" she seemed reluctant to ask.

"Someone hung him in the barn after he left you. You will be safe here tonight as Tom and I are staying here for a while, but we want to put you in protective custody." I informed her.

"I guess it's okay. I just want this to all be over, so I can stop looking over my shoulder," she said.

"Do you remember the officer who investigated the case when Bobby James died?" Tom asked.

"You mean Officer Dunning? He was a friend of Bubba's. He got them to close the case."

"Did he know Bubba had killed Bobby James?" I wanted to know.

"I don't know, but I think the two of them had some kind of family connection. They were tight," she volunteered.

"Thanks, Sally Mae; we may have more questions later." Tom turned off the tape recorder.

"What did you have planned for dinner? Maybe I can help you cook?" I suggested.

"Mike liked my fried chicken and I bought chicken breasts for tonight," she smiled as she answered.

"Why don't you just sit in the kitchen and I'll make the chicken. Do you care if I bake it?" I suggested.

"No whatever," her system was succumbing to the shock.

Tom hauled the rest of our things into the bunkhouse. He took the room at the far end of the bunkhouse and left Sally Mae and I to the other end. He did take one room on our end to set up as an office. He set up his computer, logged on, and started looking for a family connection between Jeff Dunning and Bubba Waxman.

Dinner was a quiet event. Sally Mae had several beers and then turned in. She still hadn't taken in the fact Mike was now dead and her life was still in turmoil. Tom did a check around the bunkhouse and locked all the doors.

"I think we should set up a two hour watch. I'll take the first."

"I agree, how about three hour shifts?"

"Okay, I'll wake you in three."

I walked down the hall to the room I'd sleep in. Sally Mae had closed her door and I went into the unused room. It was going to be a long night.

CHAPTER NINE

The night had been uneventful. Tom did his three hour shift and then I did mine. He did a second and by then we were both up. I started breakfast with the supplies Sally Mae had stocked in the kitchen. When she came out of the bedroom, she seemed startled to see us here.

It seemed to hit her all at once. Mike was dead and her life was in danger. She sat at the table put her head in her hands and sobbed. I wasn't sure how I felt about this. I knew she suffered a loss, I just wasn't sure how big a one considering she covered up what she knew about Bobby James' death.

I took her some coffee. "Breakfast will be ready soon."

She just gave me a blank stare and nodded. Tom took his coffee and headed for the computer. He wanted to find the family link between Jeff and Bubba. He needed to know Jeff was one of the good guys.

It explained to me why Jeff had been murdered after he talked to us. It explained why interviews had disappeared. It explained a lot and proved Mrs. Appleton had been right all along. Someone inside the department covered up a murder. Which is why it had become a cold case. What it didn't explain was why Bubba Waxman had come back from wherever he'd been. Was he behind the murders of Jeff Dunning and Mike West? Why did he think they would give him up now after all these years? How did he know the case was going to be opened again?

I gave a call to Tom and told him breakfast was ready. I set three places. He came and sat down. Sally Mae toyed with her food, ate a little, and toyed with it some more. I ate a hardy breakfast wanting to be ready for whatever the day had in store.

"You think Bubba is coming to kill me?" Sally Mae's question seemed to state the obvious.

"I think he wants to take care of loose ends," I said in all seriousness.

"Why? Why now after all these years? What does he have to gain by this?" she whined.

Tom looked at me then back a Sally Mae and answered, "We want to know, too. Keeping you here is the best way to keep you safe at the moment."

"I ain't been safe for almost sixteen years. He could have come and got me any time. Why now? What makes *now* so important? Mike and I were going to leave. We had our life all planned," she was starting to sulk.

"We don't know the answer yet, Sally Mae. Tom and I are here to work on it. We may have questions for you now and then. We may tape record some of what you say, we may not. All of this is to protect you."

"I need a shower," she said as she got up and walked down the hall.

"I don't think she's up to this. She could slip out of here at any time and try for the new life she planned."

"She's got both of us keeping an eye on her. This place is wireless for internet now so you can work where you can see her and I'll stay in the office. I'm also going to do rounds every couple of hours. I want to stagger the times so no one will see a pattern."

"Okay, Tom. I'm going to clean up from breakfast, take a survey of what food is here, and see what we need. We can shop at the all night place out on Route 15."

I took a quick inventory of the kitchen, made a list, and set it on the counter for later. Then I went to check on Sally Mae. She was curled up in her bed facing away from the door. She was crying. I thought I'd just slip out and leave her alone to her grief.

"Wait."

I stopped in the doorway and looked back.

"I don't remember your name," she said quietly.

"You can call me, Macy."

"Thank you, Macy."

"For what? I haven't done much more than question you and cook a couple of meals."

"For giving me a sense of safety I haven't felt safe in a long time," she stated simply.

"I'm glad I could be of help."

"It's more than just you being here. It was good to finally talk about what happened to Bobby James. I was so sure he'd go to the militia for the weekend. I never expected him to show up at the bar. I was just crying in my beer when Mike came in. I was surprised as I thought he was going with Bobby James. He said he really didn't believe in the militia and he didn't think Bobby James would join. He thought Bobby James was just showing off for Bubba. There we were on the dance floor, slow dancing, and in came Bobby James. It was like he was looking for a fight. I'd never seen him so mad. He was always such a gentle person. He was the first to laugh at a joke no matter how bad it was and the first to forgive someone for a mistake, but not that night. I just don't know what got into him."

"Sometimes talking can help."

"I used to think if I could go back and just talk to him I'd understand. It was his choice to go. I thought he decided I wasn't worth it. I gave him that foolish ultimatum me or the militia. I was so sure he chose the militia over me. I spent most of the night in tears. Mike had only just arrived. Bobby James would have hit him then but Bubba pulled him back. It's when he ran out and took Bubba's truck. I think it was taking his truck which made Bubba so mad. The truck was his only possession and he never let anyone drive it. I told them where he'd go. I thought if I could just reason with him things would be okay. Then Mike stepped in because he thought Bobby James would hit me. I ran then. The next thing I knew Mike was there and said he was going to take me home. I should have done something. Instead I got in the car and let Mike take me home. What was I thinking?"

"You weren't thinking; you were hurting. You just wanted to get away. It's understandable."

"What am I supposed to do now?"

"Let's make sure you're safe and then we can think about your future."

"I'm going to shower. Then I can help you with lunch."

"Sounds like a plan." I left her sitting up in the bed, hopefully feeling a little better.

Tom stood in the living room when I entered. He put his finger to his lips and motioned me to follow him. We went into the office he'd set up. He closed the door behind us.

"Macy, we have a real problem."

"I got that, what is it?"

"Bubba Waxman was Jeff Dunning's son."

"What?"

"He and his high school girlfriend, Angela Waxman had a son. He was named Jeffery Joseph Waxman. Bubba was a nickname he got at an early age and it stayed with him."

"No wonder the case went cold. How do you protect your child? You make the bad stuff go away. It's why the interviews were gone. But why did Jeff Dunning give us his notes?" I asked.

"Good question, unless he couldn't live with it anymore. I'm still trying to find out where Bubba has been holed up since Bobby James' murder."

"That's it," I suddenly knew what was nagging me about Jeff.

"What's it?" Tom asked.

"I had this niggling thing going on when we were at Dunning's. He was shocked the interviews were gone. So were all the photos of the people interviewed. It's because Bubba Waxman looked like a young Jeff. I can't believe others didn't see it."

"Maybe it's because Jeff was a widower with no kids. Molly had been the love of his life or so everyone thought. She was on her way to work one morning and her car was plowed into by a drunk. They could not save her. Jeff was devastated. No one ever thought he might have had a child with someone else in a different town."

"But it was his face," I said, "I should have seen it then."

"It was different sixteen years ago. People didn't look for family resemblance. We didn't know there was any connection between Bubba and Jeff. Why would we?"

"I see what you're saying. Did you find anything else out about his early life?"

"Seems when he learned his father was a police officer, he did everything he could to get into trouble. He became the proverbial bad boy. Mostly minor scrapes and his mother made sure he earned the money to repay people for things he broke or destroyed."

"Seems like his mother tried to keep him in line."

"She lived with her parents. The mother died just after Bubba started school. Her father didn't take the pregnancy well and died not knowing who Bubba's father was. She seemed to be protecting Dunning too."

"Couldn't have been easy for her."

"No, Bubba was a good student until about the eighth grade; his grades dropped off that year and continued to fall off until he dropped out at sixteen."

"Wonder when he learned who his father was," I pondered aloud.

"I don't know. I'm going to make a run to Hillside and see if I can talk to his mother. From what I can tell she still lives there."

"When are you going to go?"

"I'll wait until after lunch and take the rental. I'll pick up groceries in Hillside on my way back. Do you have a list?"

"Sure do." I moved to get the list. I found Sally Mae in the kitchen getting ready to make lunch.

She looked up and smiled. "Hope you don't mind I put some soup on. I can make some grilled cheese sandwiches to go with it."

"Sounds great did you see the grocery list?"

Sally Mae reached down beside her and picked it up. "I hope you don't mind I added a few things."

"No problem, whatever we need. Tom is going to question someone and will pick the things up on the way back. We want to draw as little attention to ourselves as possible."

"Then he'll want to come in the back way and not by the house."

"There is a back way in here? Tom."

Tom joined us.

Sally Mae explained about the back way into the bunkhouse and told us it was how she got here.

"You have a car here?" I asked.

"Yes."

"Show us," Tom said heading for the front door.

"Not that way," Sally Mae said.

Tom stopped.

Sally Mae was heading for the back door; the way we had seen her come in the day before. We followed. Sally Mae led the way to a lean-to a short walk from the back door. It was surrounded by brush and neither of us had seen it the night before. Sally Mae's car was parked inside. She had pulled brush up around it to help obscure it from view.

From here, Tom could see the lane leading to the road. He helped and we put more brush around Sally Mae's car. It wouldn't be going anyplace for a while. Then Tom went to get the rental car. He left by way of Mrs. Appleton's driveway, but would not be returning the same way again.

The driveway by the house should not show any more activity than it would in a normal day. We didn't want anyone to know there was a chance we could be here. Sally Mae had been very helpful in making that happen.

She and I walked back to the bunkhouse. The soup would be ready and we needed to make the sandwiches. Tom had decided to pick something up on the way to Hillside. He was looking forward to interviewing Angela Waxman about her son.

CHAPTER TEN

Sally Mae and I had lunch and cleaned up the dishes. She took herself off to the bedroom. The next thing I knew she was carrying a load of laundry in a basket.

"Is there a washer and dryer here?"

"Yes." She walked toward the office and opened what I had assumed was a closet. Inside were an apartment sized washer and dryer. She sorted the laundry and began a wash. "Do you need to throw anything in?"

"No, thanks I should have added laundry soap to the list."

"I did."

"Someone was thinking ahead. Did I miss anything else?"

"Nothing from what I could see. So, why are you the one stuck babysitting me?"

"I'm not stuck. Tom found some information on Bubba while he was on the computer. Do you know anything about his family?"

"Not really. He drifted into town and started hanging with Mike and Bobby James. Bobby James thought he was so cool. He was older and so Bobby James thought he was wiser. I didn't much like him. Seemed like he was always trying to come between Bobby James and me, as if he wanted Bobby James all to himself. He finally ended it for us once and for all."

She hung her head. I didn't know if she was sorry it had ended or if she was just feeling sorry for herself.

"Why couldn't he leave Mike alone? Mike wouldn't have hurt anyone."

"I don't know the answer. I do know he is looking good for three murders. I need to do some research and see if I can find out where he has been for the past few years. Do you have any ideas?"

"I'd check all the jails and prisons. He lit out right after the funeral. He didn't even come to the hall for dinner. He was just gone. I haven't seen or heard from him since. It wasn't until Mike came to the apartment the other night and said we had to stage a fight."

"Are you going to be alright if I work on this? I could bring the laptop into the living room."

"You don't have to. I was thinking of doing some baking. I bake when things go wrong. It's probably why I'm not as thin as I used to be." Her bitter laugh said more to me than her words.

"Okay, the door is open feel free to come in when you are done. Make sure you don't unlock the doors."

"I'm not letting anyone in. In fact, I'll be hightailing it to find you if I even suspect there is anyone near a door or window so fast you won't know what happened."

I smiled and sat at the computer. I heard her walk toward the kitchen. Then I was deep into the police files in Hillside. If he wasn't here, did he go home? Did he get into trouble there? It was a starting place. I'd been at it for over an hour, the smells from the kitchen were making me hungry. Then Sally Mae appeared at my side with a steaming cup of coffee. She also brought cream and sugar.

"I couldn't remember if you took these in your coffee."

"I don't often drink coffee, but I'll take both in mine."

"If you'd like I can go make some tea. I drink tea so there are tea bags here."

"This will do for now. It smells wonderful, what did you make?"

"I made some French bread so we can have it with dinner. I also made a surprise dessert and the coffee cake for breakfast is almost done."

"How did you manage to accomplish it in just an hour?"

"An hour? You've been at this for almost three hours. Did you find anything useful?"

"I might have."

I heard someone at the door.

"You stay here." I left the room pulling the door closed softly behind me. I unholstered my gun, hoping I wouldn't have to use it. Tom was coming in the back door arms loaded with groceries. I quickly holstered my weapon, called to Sally Mae to let her know it was okay, and went to help Tom.

"What smells so good?"

"Sally Mae bakes when she is stressed."

"Wonderful."

Sally Mae had come out and was helping us to put things away. Then she shooed us both out of the kitchen as she took the cinnamon coffee cake from the oven and set it on the cooling rack.

She quickly started preparing dinner.

Tom locked the back door and we went into the office.

"What did you learn?"

"Angela Waxman has had a hard life. Her father never let her forget she was unmarried and the mother of a bastard. She didn't say it, but I get the feeling he beat her on a regular basis. She's been a waitress at a local restaurant since shortly after Bubba was born. She continues to work there. She tried to keep him out of trouble. He found some papers once which made him ask questions about his father. She told the boy he was a decorated policeman. Bubba could not understand why if he was so decorated and highly thought of he would have abandoned his responsibilities toward them. Angela couldn't make him understand. He set about getting into trouble in the hopes of identifying his father."

"Wow, negative attention is better than no attention."

"Something along those lines. He'd been an honor student up until eighth grade. She's not sure if it was when he learned about his father or if it came later. Her father didn't help. He kept telling Bubba he'd never amount to anything. We know some kids live up to the expectations set for them. She didn't come right out and say it, but I got the impression he beat the boy as often as he beat her."

"So, has she seen him recently?"

"Bubba went to visit her right after the murder of Bobby James. He was broken up over the death of his friend and said he needed to get away for a while. Angela has an uncle in Kentucky she sent him to. She was hoping he could straighten his life out there. She didn't hear much until her uncle called to say he'd been arrested and would need a lawyer. Angela drove down as soon as she could with her life savings in her purse. It seems Bubba had been in a bar fight and had killed the other person. He was given a plea agreement and pled guilty to voluntary manslaughter. He was given six to twelve years. He was released about three weeks ago and made his way home."

"So what brought him here?"

"Angela said he kept talking about some friends here he needed to look up. He'd also told her he'd like to see his father again. Angela didn't know the two had ever met. Which was all she could tell me. She has not seen him since."

"Did she know the name of his friends?"

"No, and she hadn't known this is where Jeff Dunning lived. She was distraught to hear Dunning had been murdered. Dunning had sent her a regular check from the time he left her until he retired from the force. In the last check, he told her he was retiring and would not be able to keep paying. She never heard from him again. He never indicated he met his son."

"Was she shocked to know we are looking at him for murder?"

"She seemed resigned. Like I said, her life has not been easy. She is still living in her parents' house. The décor was probably set by her mother and has not changed her entire life. She does not know what to do with this son she lost along the way."

"Well we can log into the Kentucky prison system and see if we can find out what kind of prisoner he was. It would be nice to know if he was let out on good behavior or served his entire sentence."

"Let's do it after dinner. I then need to type up a report and forward it on to the captain."

We headed for the kitchen where Sally Mae had made lasagna and was working on a salad. I found dishes and set the table. Tom had purchased a bottle of wine which he opened so it could breathe. Sally Mae made garlic butter to go on the French bread loaf she made earlier. It was going to be a meal fit for kings.

CHAPTER ELEVEN

With dinner out of the way, Sally Mae finished folding her clothes. I made a circuit of the area around the bunkhouse and out to check on the cars in the lean-to. Once inside I secured the doors and settled down. Sally Mae had found something on TV to watch. It was some show on brides with no manners. I couldn't imagine why anyone would want to film this much less watch it. I went to the kitchen to make some tea. Sally Mae was instantly at my side.

"If you want to go get Tom, I can serve dessert."

"Sure, he might want some coffee."

"I'll get it started."

I walked slowly down the hall toward our makeshift office. Tom had just finished sending off his report to the captain. I let him know we had dessert and he was on his feet instantly.

Back in the kitchen everything was on the table and Sally Mae was back on the sofa watching the tube. She only set out two plates.

"Aren't you having any?"

"No, I bake but I never eat the desserts."

Tom and I quietly ate the apple pie she baked. It was delicious. I was puzzled because earlier she mentioned that her weight was from eating her own baking. Now she said she didn't eat desserts. Something was going on with her. Tom was taking the first watch so I did up the dishes and headed to bed. Sally Mae followed along.

When the lights were out, Sally Mae decided she wanted to talk. She came into my room and sat on the other bed.

"Macy, do you think Mike knew Bubba was dangerous? Could he have been trying to protect me?"

"I do believe so, yes. Why do you ask?"

"I knew Mike was sweet on me back when I was dating Bobby James. I also knew he'd never do anything to destroy the friendship. I never meant to flirt with him at the bar, seems if I just ignored him like usual none of this would have happened. Bobby James and I would be married and have kids. We might have even divorced, but they would still be hanging out either way. Do you have any regrets in your life?"

"Many and unlike you there is no way I can fix any of mine. You have a chance to make it right for Bobby James' mother. You can give Mike justice when you testify about what happened that night, and how Mike came to your rescue last Sunday night. You can fix some of your regrets. I never can."

"Why can't you? Just talk to the people. You should be able to fix things too."

"The people I need to talk to are dead or incapacitated. I can't say all the things I didn't."

Sally Mae fell silent as she pondered what Macy told her. She lay down on the bed. I listened to her breathing until I knew she was a sleep. Then I rolled over to wrestle with my own demons and tried to get some sleep. I would be on duty in three hours.

When I took over for Tom, he moved his laptop into the living room. He found Bubba had served eight years of his sentence. He had not always been the model inmate. Frequently he spent time in solitary confinement after brawls. The guards could never say he instigated them, but they had their suspicions. We had now accounted for about all of Bubba's time away.

What brought him to Rivers Edge again? Why was it so important he find Mike and Sally Mae? What was his current beef with Jeff? Why were Mike and Jeff dead? Did Bubba kill them?

We still had too many questions and not enough answers. I thought I would probe the computer and see if I could find anything else. Tom made one more trip outside to make sure the area was secure. When he entered he looked spooked.

He motioned me to douse the lights. I did so quickly. I unholstered my weapon and moved slowly away from the back door. I headed toward the bedroom where Sally Mae lay sleeping. My first instinct was to protect her. Then I would back up my partner. Tom nodded as if reading my mind.

I needed to wake her quietly and get her someplace safe. I placed my hand over her mouth and leaned in to whisper.

"Sally Mae." She startled awake but calmed when she saw it was me. "Be real quiet. We may have someone outside. I need to get you hidden."

Sally Mae nodded, but even in the dark I could see the fear in her eyes. I moved my hand away from her mouth. She pointed to the rug. I looked at her questioning.

"There's a basement hidden under the rug. Mike wanted me to be safe. It is stocked with food, water, and blankets for six months."

We quickly rolled the rug back. She showed me how to open the door, and then went down the stairs. She had a light on and was making herself hidden as I lowered the door and put the rug back in place. I made my way back toward the living room. Tom had turned the table sideways to use as a shield. He also upended the coffee table, put sofa cushions near it and the chair cushions near the table. He motioned me to take the table and prepare for a firefight. We just waited. I heard scratching at the back door then nothing. I glanced out the kitchen window and burst out laughing.

"Macy, what the hell are you laughing about?"

By this time I was on my feet, totally unprotected, and pointing at the window. Framed in it was a black bear. Tom too began laughing. Our intruder turned out to have four legs not two. I quickly went back to let Sally Mae know we were safe.

The rest of the night was uneventful. Tom and I took our three-hour shifts and Sally Mae returned to her bed. Morning seemed to come too soon.

CHAPTER TWELVE

I awoke to the smell of bacon cooking. When I rolled over I saw Sally Mae was still sleeping. I quietly pulled on my robe and headed for the kitchen. Tom was standing at the stove. The coffee was ready so I took a cup.

"I take it there is nothing new on our friend?"

"You mean the four legged one or Bubba?"

"Either one," I said shrugging.

"No. The four-legged one evidently found food. He did attempt to get into the trash can. We need to be real careful if we are going to continue doing outside checks."

"I think we can let the outside checks go. At least we know we can be prepared at a moments' notice. I'd like to explore the little hidden room later," my curiosity came through in my comment.

"Yeah, me too. Are scrambled eggs okay with you?"

"Sure, do I have time for a quick shower?"

"If you can shower in ten minutes then yes."

It took me less than ten minutes to shower and change. By then Sally Mae was up, had her first cup of coffee, and was making toast. Tom had the eggs cooking. I set the table and we were ready to start the day.

"Did you find out anything yesterday which would help?" Sally Mae asked as we sat down to eat.

"I found out some of what makes Bubba tick, but we are no closer to locating him."

"I haven't seen him since the funeral, so I'm not sure I would even know him," Sally Mae added as if to say she wouldn't be much help to us.

"Did he make any passes at you back then?"

"No, why do you ask?" she looked at Tom with a puzzled expression.

"Just trying to figure out what made him want to come back here," Tom answered.

I listened hoping I'd pick up something helpful.

"I don't recall him dating anyone special back then. He ignored me or treated me as if I was his own private slave. He would order me to bring him beer or get myself to the kitchen. It was creepy. I hated the nights Bobby James would invite him to be with us. He never brought a girl," Sally Mae was remembering again, she had a faraway expression on her face.

"What made it creepy?"

"It was like he wanted to make me seem worthless. He never used my name, just called me, woman or girl."

"I bet it's what his grandfather called his mother. He was treating you the way he believed women were supposed to be treated."

"Well, *that's* just sick," Sally Mae said indignantly her face mirroring disgust.

We finished breakfast; Sally Mae did the dishes and put them away. Tom and I went to work in the office. We learned Bubba showed up at Jeff's when he was sixteen. He had petitioned to put Bubba on his insurance. At the time he had shown guardianship papers for a nephew, one Jeffery Joseph Waxman. He added the boy and carried health insurance on him until he was nineteen. Since he was not in school, he could no longer be covered by the insurance.

"If he had his son with him why did he keep paying the child support?" I asked. This puzzled me.

"Maybe he felt guilty for leaving them behind? Maybe he knew what Angela's father was like?" Tom replied. "We'll probably never know."

I was sure it might be part of it. I wondered if Bubba had found a way to blackmail Jeff into continuing. It was something to think about. He managed to get all his minor scrapes taken care of by using Jeff's influence as a police officer. He might stoop to blackmail.

My next couple of questions might have interesting answers. "Do you know who Jeff left his worldly belongings to?"

"I checked during the night. The will was filed in probate, but they had not notified the beneficiaries yet. I'm putting in a call to his attorney this morning."

"Okay. Do you think Bubba knew who would benefit?"

"It would just be a guess on my part and I doubt he cared. Money has never seemed to be what motivates him. I think he was miserable and wanted to make others miserable," there was contempt in Tom's voice when he answered.

"Have we found anything which might tell us where he is?" I asked.

"Not so far. Sally Mae doesn't seem to know either."

I went to stretch my legs. I was not getting near enough exercise. Tom was calling Jeff's attorney. I needed to do something, but just didn't know what. Something was nagging at me. I knew I was missing something. Walking helps me think, so I went to check the cars in the lean-to. They were still covered. I circled behind the bunkhouse and moved the garbage can. I could see where the bear had been. Finally I went to check on my car. It was well covered. It was then I discovered the mound with the grate over it. What was this and where did it lead?

I pulled the grate and it came away easily. I flipped on my flashlight and headed into what appeared to be a tunnel used recently. I kept going and the tunnel widened. I found cases of canned food, water and supplies. There was a light switch. I flipped it on and the room lit up. There I found a generator and gas to run it. Soon I found a door which opened easily. I slowly went in. I found myself in what looked like a safe room. There were two beds, a small hot plate, a refrigerator, microwave and supplies for several months. I made my way to a stairway. I slowly climbed the stairs to another door. I banged on the door when I could not open it. After a few minutes the door opened Sally Mae and Tom were staring down at me.

"Well, this is no longer a safe hide away," I commented.

"How did you get down there?" Tom asked.

"You two had better come down and see what I've found."

They made their way down the stairs. This was the same place I'd hidden Sally Mae when we thought that Bubba was outside. She thought she was safe and so did I. We now knew there was a second storage chamber and an outside entrance. We needed to find a way to secure this entrance or Bubba would be able to sneak in at anytime.

"This is not good," Tom said. "I'll see if I can come up with a way to hide this entrance."

"We also need a way to lock that second door. It's nice to know there is an exit if we need it."

"Mike never told me about this," Sally Mae said looking around in awe.

"I figured he didn't or you would have run last night," I said truthfully.

"I have no reason to run from you. Both of you have been nothing but kind and have made me feel safe."

"You two go inside, I'll work on hiding this entrance," Tom was looking serious about making this area safe.

Sally Mae and I retraced our steps back into the bedroom. This was a new twist. Tom might need to install a dead bolt on the inside of the door so we didn't receive any unwanted visitors.

I had also been thinking about Bubba. We knew he killed in the heat of the moment when he was angry. He was angry with Bobby James for taking his truck, his prized possession; it resulted in Bobby James being beaten almost to death. But was Bubba the one who pulled the trigger? He killed a guy in a bar fight afterward and done time. What caused him to kill Mike? Mike was not beaten in the heat of the moment. Someone took time to make it look as though he committed suicide. What exactly was the motive? Who had wanted him dead? Then there was Jeff. His neck broken then shot with his own weapon. Neither of these murders fit with Bubba's MO (modus operandi). Someone else had to be behind these two murders. Which meant Tom and I were in more trouble than we thought. I briefed Tom when he came in. We decided it was time to check in with the captain.

CHAPTER THIRTEEN

Once the captain had been briefed we sat at the kitchen table trying to decide what to look at next. Sally Mae made a fresh pot of coffee and a cup of tea for me. Sally Mae wanted us to get her some nail polish and a couple of romance novels. She was getting bored just watching TV. I could understand. I wanted some yarn and crochet hooks, making an afghan was good for keeping me occupied. We also needed to get a dead bolt for the inside door of the safe room. I was not keen of the idea of night visitors. We also needed a small corkboard. We had two new murders to figure out and we needed to get a lead on Bubba.

Now that we had our list and some kind of plan, Tom decided I should be the one to go out. I would be able to get a dead bolt at any hardware store. I knew what kind of yarn and hooks to get, be able to pick out nail polish, and some romance books for Sally Mae. He and the captain were going to stay in close contact. The captain would be delivering a package to Mrs. Appleton for us and Tom wanted to be close by when it arrived.

Sally Mae said she'd make some lunch and check supplies. She didn't think we'd need anything now because we knew there were plenty of supplies in the "hold" as she called it. She put together a quick lunch of soup and sandwiches then I was on my way.

I decided I didn't want to be seen in Rivers Edge so I took the road north out of town. It was going to be thirty miles to the next town but I was sure I could shop there without running into anyone. I was right. The town had a Wal-Mart and I was able to do one stop shopping.

I bought a dozen different nail polishes and two bottles of polish remover along with four books two by Fern Michaels, one by Nora Roberts which was a trilogy, and one by Catherine Coulter in her FBI series. Just for something different, I picked up *People Magazine* and *Oprah Magazine* as well as *The National Enquirer*. I found the dead bolt easily then headed to the yarn section. I threw in two dozen skeins of yarn and picked up a size G hook. I could make several afghans out of what I had. Since I didn't know how long we'd be hidden away I wanted to be prepared. I also picked up the few things Sally Mae had added to our food list and was on my way back. I managed to get everything and not see anyone I knew.

Back at the bunkhouse, Tom was setting up make shift two corkboards in our living room since we had outgrown the office area. One would be for Mike West; the other would be for Jeff Dunning. We had to find the connection to these two men to find our killer. The one thing we knew for sure was Bubba didn't do it. These were both crimes of opportunity and they had to be linked somehow.

Bubba was a creature of habit. Tom decided to dress down and hit the local bar. He'd just check it out and see if Bubba showed up. Maybe if he was lucky he'd get to talk to him. For now he was just planning to watch and follow. He'd play it by ear when he got there. I wasn't happy about him going in without back up. He assured me that back up was taken care of the captain was providing back up. He planned to be in the parking lot.

"And if something goes bad inside, how is the captain going to be of help?" I asked worry on my face.

"I think I can handle myself," was Tom's curt reply.

I didn't like it but I didn't see any options. Tom had the release photo taken of Bubba in Kentucky. He probably let his hair get longer. He was never been one to wear a beard, but there was always a first time. Once we knew where Bubba was staying, the captain would pass information on the two murders to Tom and he would return here. The captain was going to keep watch until morning. We could not tail Bubba 24/7, but we would know where he spent his nights.

Sally Mae had put a pot roast into the crock-pot earlier in the day. While Tom and I were setting up the corkboards and discussing what would be going down tonight, she had been busy in the kitchen.

"Hey, you two, dinner is ready," Sally Mae announced.

She had added a salad and rolls to our fare and there was left over pie from the previous night. I helped Sally Mae set the table while Tom got into his casual clothes. He did the spiky thing with his hair and put on a skin tight black t-shirt with a flannel shirt over it. He had on western boots and put a gold chain around his neck. If he didn't scream redneck, nothing would. He headed out the back door to the rental car and took off down the road. He and the captain had set a meeting place in an alley behind the hardware store. It was out of my hands now.

Sally Mae went to the bedroom and I could smell the nail polish she opened. When she came out twenty minutes later she asked, "You want me to do your nails?"

"I'm not really a nail polish girl. I tend to bite my nails."

"Well, then let's do your toes. What color do you like?"

In spite of myself I warmed to the idea and Sally Mae quickly went to work polishing my toes in a candy apple red. We talked about her career as a beautician while she worked.

"What made you give it up?" I asked, curious.

"I always wanted my own shop. It seemed like I was always working for someone else. I kept taking classes so I could do more than just hair. I learned to do nails and pedicures. Nothing seemed to help. I was always paying rent for my station and barely clearing enough to live on. So I started tending bar after hours. The bar tending and waitressing brought in more money. I started spending more time doing on those jobs. I still love hairdressing but I don't see much future in it. Especially now Mike is gone."

"Sally Mae, did Mike have a will?"

"I don't know. I just figured it would all go to his mom."

"Okay, it's something we need to know. I'll get the captain on it in the morning unless it's in the stuff he gives to Tom later tonight."

"Other than when Bobby James died did you ever have any reason to see Jeff Dunning?"

"No, he pretty much left me alone after the case got closed."

"Did Mike ever talk about seeing him or talking to him?"

"Not that I can remember. Why are you asking?" Sally Mae seemed confused.

I was looking at the board. So far the only link between the two murdered men was the Bobby James Appleton case.

"I was just trying to figure out if there was something between them we might have overlooked."

She nodded, told me I couldn't walk anywhere for a while until my polish dried, and took her tools to the bedroom. When she came back she was carrying a book. She curled up in an armchair and began to read.

I was still looking at the boards. We didn't have enough information to make any of my theories work. What connected the two men besides Bobby James? Who would have wanted them both dead? Who would have us believe Bubba was behind it? These were the questions Tom and I would have to answer and we needed solid evidence to back it up. An hour later I gave up, took out some yarn and began making a ripple afghan. It was a pattern I used so many times I didn't need the instructions front of me anymore. I worked on it long after Sally Mae went to bed waiting for Tom to return.

CHAPTER FOURTEEN

I awoke to the sound of the door opening. I reached behind me for my gun. I opened my eyes, sat up quickly with my gun forward in a ready position. Tom was stopped in his tracks.

"It's okay, Macy, it's just me," he assured me.

I holstered my gun and was quick to rise.

"I'm sorry, Tom. I didn't mean to fall asleep. How did it go?"

I moved to the kitchen to make a fresh pot of coffee and a cup of tea. I wanted to know everything.

"I met the captain. He handed me some papers and I called him on my cell leaving the line open so he could hear everything, just in case I had a problem with Bubba. I took a corner table, ordered a beer, and just watched people. I was about to give up when Bubba strolled in. He looked the place over, ordered two beers and headed for my table. You would have thought he knew I was waiting for him. He asked if he could sit with me and offered me the other beer. He sat down, introducing himself as Bubba and offered his hand. I took it and told him I was Tom. He said he hadn't seen me there before. I told him I was new in town and heard it was a good place. He agreed.

"We had a few more beers and I told him I had to get up in the morning. I needed to find a job. I asked if he knew anyone hiring, he didn't, but said he would keep an ear out for me and next time I could buy the drinks.

"I walked out to my car and waited for him to come out. It didn't take long. He hopped into a beat up truck and was out of the lot. I followed him to a rundown part of town. He parked in front of an old house, walked up the front stairs, and went inside. I kept driving. The captain stayed to keep a watch on him. I'll get a call in the morning from the captain to see if he stayed there or had picked me up as a tail and left once I drove by."

"You didn't pick up anything useful while talking to him?" I was eager to know everything.

"No, we mostly talked beer and women. He doesn't have much use for women."

"This was not as productive as we expected," I sighed.

"No, but it's gotten us closer to him."

"I looked at the two boards while you were out. The murders were both murders of opportunity. Bubba's murder was in the heat of the moment. I'm afraid we have two killers to worry about. This is not going to be as easy as we thought."

"Macy, if you don't mind I want to call it a day. The captain is going to call early and I want to get to the package he sent. We might find something in there. We should go over Jeff's notes again, too. It might hold something we overlooked."

I took our cups to the kitchen and put them in the sink. I turned off the coffee pot and turned out the light. Tom had already headed toward his room. I made my way to the room Sally decided to share with me. She had fallen asleep reading. I doused the light, put on my pajamas and crawled into bed. My last thought before sleep was we were nowhere near closing the case.

CHAPTER FIFTEEN

Sally Mae was in the kitchen when I wandered in the next morning. She had breakfast underway. Tom was still sleeping. "Did Tom have a successful night?" she asked.

"He did except I almost blew his head off when he got back." Sally Mae looked at me in horror. "Some security I am. I almost shot him because I fell asleep."

"You should have come to bed. I think we're safe here," she admonished.

"We will be unless Bubba decides to follow Tom."

"I hadn't thought about that. Tom was able to find him then?" curiosity laced her question.

She handed me a cup of tea, took a cup for herself, and poured herself some coffee. "I hope you don't mind oatmeal this morning. I was in the mood for something different. I added raisins to it. It should be ready in a minute," she said as she started dishing it into bowls.

"It sounds fine to me. You don't need to keep cooking for us. Both Tom and I are capable of cooking."

"I know, but it gives me something to do and makes me feel part of what you are doing. I'd be happy to do any laundry you need done, too."

Tom came in just then. "Good morning, ladies. What have we got for breakfast this morning?"

"Oatmeal with raisins. Hope it's okay?" Sally Mae answered. She turned to reach for a cup and poured coffee for Tom.

He took the cup and we all headed to the table. Sally Mae brought steaming bowls of oatmeal, and then went back for milk and brown sugar. There wasn't much conversation over breakfast.

Tom's cell phone rang breaking the silence. He looked at the number and answered, "Maxwell."

Sally Mae and I could only hear Tom's side of the conversation. "Yes."

"I see."

"I'll check it out. Thanks." He hung up the phone and smiled at both of us.

Finally I said, "Well?"

"It was Bubba. He says he heard they were hiring at the local hardware store. He's also found a lead on a job at a gas station doing oil changes."

"Wow! Fast work," I was surprised at the caller's identity.

"Yeah, since the gas station is the one Bobby James worked at and the hardware store position was Mike's."

"How did he know to call you?" Sally Mae asked.

"He and I met at the bar you last saw him at. I figured he'd hit his old stomping grounds. We talked and I was able to follow him to where he is staying. My captain kept watch on him all night. He didn't leave. The captain had them run the address to come up with the owners. The house is a rundown rental. It's rented by Lacy Ann Stockton."

"Lacy Ann Stockton," Sally Mae practically shouted the name. "She was hanging on Bubba's arm for a while when we were kids. She married some guy a few years back. They got a divorce when he beat her and she lost the baby she was carrying. I never heard what happened to her after. Why would she want to be with Bubba?"

"I'm sure we don't know. I'm also just as certain, we will know before the sun sets," Tom answered her. I was wondering if she was jealous.

I had been thinking since I got up and I had an idea to toss at Tom. "So, who was Jeff's partner on the Appleton case?"

"Drew Riley, I believe. I'll check. Why do you ask?"

"Then he would be the other person connected to Bobby James, Mike, and Jeff. What do you know about him?" My mind was churning with possibilities.

"Not much. He still works on the force. He's an ex-marine. His wife left him and took their two girls. He's pretty much a loner. Would rather do patrol than work as a detective. Why?"

"Could he have taken the interviews? Could he be the insider person Bubba has and not Jeff?"

"I guess anything is possible. What do you want to do?" Tom asked.

"When you talk to the captain, I want to be able to read the man's IA (internal affairs) file. I want to know everything about him."

"I'll ask him. Don't know what you think we'll find, but I'll ask," he assured me.

"I don't know what we'll find either, but I want to cover all the bases. This might be the something we are missing.

I stood and took my bowl and cup to the kitchen. Sally Mae grabbed hers and Tom's and joined me.

"I've got the dishes," she said quietly.

I nodded and went to get dressed for the day.

CHAPTER SIXTEEN

I was puzzled about Tom. I thought he'd see what I was getting at with my interest in Drew Riley. It should have been obvious. Riley was the one person who was tied to all three deaths. I took my laptop and sat on my bed. I was going to do some digging on my own. If my suspicions were right we could be in more danger than we thought.

If Drew Riley was an ex-marine, he could easily break a neck. It didn't matter he might be older. Both Mike and Jeff had no reason to believe he was a threat to them. They wouldn't have suspected they were in danger. His coming up behind them wouldn't have caused any concern with either man. It would explain Jeff having a beer with him. It could also mean Bubba was in some serious trouble. I needed to be armed when we made the case against Riley and if Tom wasn't thrilled about going after a fellow officer, I wasn't taking any chances.

I pulled up the site I went to for credit checks. I ran one for Drew Riley. I needed to know if he was living above his means. Did he have cash no one knew about? Then I was going to find out all I could about the ex-Mrs. Riley and where she was. I had my work cut out for me.

I didn't even notice Sally Mae come in until she set a cup of tea down next to me. I looked up then and said, "Thanks."

"I get the feeling you and Tom are on opposite sides of something, I'm just not sure what the something is," she hesitated waiting for me to respond.

"Well if my hunch is right, we may be in more danger than we first thought. Bubba may also be in danger. Tom's wife is expecting and the danger to him could spill over to her and the boys. It's not so much we are on the opposite sides as it is we both have our own theories of what is going on," I explained.

"Have you been partners long?" again her curiosity was making her ask questions.

"I've been in Rivers Edge about ten years, but Tom has only been my partner for six of those. Why do you ask?"

"Well you seem comfortable together, but I know you ain't sleeping with him."

"Why would you think we were lovers?" I chuckled.

"I guess I've watched too much TV, but I always thought male and female partners ended up together."

"I see. I guess I should watch more TV. Tom and Shannon have been married about fifteen years. They have two boys and are hoping for a girl this time. Their relationship is solid. I would never want to try to get in between them. I envy what they have."

"So where is the man in your life?" she wanted to know.

I was taken aback but only for a moment. It was natural for Sally Mae to want to know about the people protecting her.

"My fiancé died in the line of duty two years before I moved to Rivers Edge. I've been too busy working to have a social life," I gave her the standard answer when the truth was, I was horribly lonely.

"Girl, you must get very lonely. We women need our men, too. I could show you the night life when this is over." Then she laughed before saying, "Like you would want to hang out with an old lady like me. Seriously, you need to start thinking about you. You're young you can still have a family."

"I guess. Right now I just want to get this case solved." I was uncomfortable with her questions.

"There's always going to be a case to solve. You need to start looking out for you."

I laughed and told her I'd take that under advisement. Then I took a sip of tea and went back to my laptop. Sally Mae curled up on her bed with another one of the books I bought for her. I was impressed she spent so much time reading and not just the gossip columns.

I had a lot to think about on top of the case. Instead Sally Mae's comments lingered in my head as I searched through Drew Riley's financial records. So far everything seemed to be on the up and up. It was then I discovered something I'd not seen before. I left the room and went to the office and connected my laptop to the printer. I clicked print and papers began spewing out of the printer. I thought I had my smoking gun.

When the printer was done I went in search of Tom. We had something to talk about now. We would also have a lot more digging to do if what I suspected was true.

Tom was making himself a sandwich. He asked if I wanted one. I told him I'd wait. I had something for him to look at.

"Well, Macy, that makes two of us. I finally got through the information the captain gave me yesterday. I need to rethink my first theory."

"Let's see if it coincides with my theory. Then we'll have a better idea of what to do next."

Tom made his way to the table, "Okay what have you got?"

I handed him the pages I'd just printed. I made a cup of tea while he read and ate. I knew when he was done we'd have another discussion of our options. I started making a sandwich for myself. Tom would need time to come to the conclusions I'd drawn.

Sally Mae wandered into the kitchen and I offered to make her a sandwich. She accepted and poured herself a cup of coffee while I made a second sandwich. She sat on the couch and turned on the TV. She found a noon news show. It was almost as if watching the news would help her to be part of the world outside the bunkhouse.

I handed her a plate with a sandwich on it and took my plate to the table. Tom was almost finished with his sandwich and the pages I had printed. I could tell by the frown on his face he didn't like what he was reading.

Tom looked up. "I need to take a walk. This is not good. We'll talk when I come back." He took his plate and cup to the sink and went out the back door of the bunkhouse.

I was more than puzzled. Did Tom know something I didn't? Was he somehow connected to Drew Riley? I'd thought what I found would bring him to my way of thinking. It seemed to have driven us farther apart.

Just then the announcer on the news said, "This just in, two local detectives are missing. Tom Maxwell and his partner Macy McVannel have not reported for work since the day Jeff Dunning was murdered. Where are the two officers? How are they connected to Jeff Dunning? We hope to have an update on News 6 at six."

I was up and out the back door before Sally Mae could ask any questions. I needed to find Tom. If people started focusing on us Jeff's murder would fall to the back burner. We would be in serious danger from his killer.

Tom was coming back from the lean-to. He came up short as he saw me racing forward.

"Macy, what's happened? Where is Sally Mae?"

I stopped and caught my breath before I replied, "They have us on the news as missing. They hope to have an update on the news at six. Call your wife, tell her we are fine, and to lock her doors. Then call the captain. We are in a real mess. He's got a leak in the department, a leak who's trying to smoke us out."

Tom started dialing before I was done with my explanation. I turned and started back for the bunkhouse. I needed to know Sally Mae was still safe inside. I hope we hadn't been followed and put ourselves in danger. We were going to have to act soon on what we knew.

CHAPTER SEVENTEEN

S ally Mae was standing in the doorway of the bunkhouse. Tom yelled, "Get inside." We both raced to the door. Sally Mae stepped back so we could get through. Once inside with the door was locked again I took a moment to catch my breath.

"What? Did you see someone?" Sally Mae asked anxiously. I could see fear on her face.

"It was the news," I gasped.

"Oh, you and Tom are missing? It's not true your captain knows where you are."

"Yes, he does. However the person who leaked this doesn't," Tom explained. "That is the person we have to fear, who is looking for us, and poses a threat."

"Why on earth is this happening?" Her voice was rising to a panic level. "How can you to protect me?"

"Sit down, Sally Mae." Tom waited until she sat. "The only person who knows we are here is Mrs. Appleton. She doesn't know you are here. We needed someplace to hide out and thought she'd have a barn not in use. It was a bonus for us that Mike had finished fixing up the bunkhouse. It was just luck Mike had hidden you here. We will protect you to the best of our abilities."

"I thought you knew I was here and were protecting me from the person who killed Mike," she continued on the verge of hysteria.

"We didn't know until you came in, you had been living here. We thought you'd run off but took it upon ourselves to keep you from ending up like Mike," I answered trying to calm her down as my own breathing once again became normal.

"This is strange. I thought Bubba was Mike's killer. I thought he killed Mike because of Bobby James," she was calmer now, but still confused by what she was learning.

"We thought so at first," I said. "Then we learned both Mike and Jeff had their necks broken and their deaths were made to look like suicides. It is not how Bubba has killed in the past he used his fists."

"Has Bubba killed someone besides Bobby James?" I could see panic returning to her face.

Tom answered, "Yes, he did time in Kentucky for killing a man in a bar fight."

She gasped. Things were happening too fast for her to grasp all at once. Tom looked at the papers he left on the table. He looked at me as he picked them up.

"Sally Mae, you might want to spend some time in the bedroom. Macy and I are going to uncover the boards and see how her information fits. I think she could be right and we are hiding from a police officer. Which makes everything much more dangerous."

"If you don't mind, I'd like to listen. I've lived here all my life and I know a lot of secrets."

Tom looked at me and I nodded. It sure couldn't hurt. Sally Mae had been here longer than either one of us. She might be able to tell us something. We went to work setting up the boards. We put them side by side so we could put up the profiles of Bobby James, Mike, and Jeff. It didn't take long. Sally Mae had poured herself another cup of coffee and sat at the kitchen table watching. If she was surprised to see her photo go up under Bobby James and Mike she said nothing.

"Okay, Macy, get your yellow pad. I want to recap what we know. You can put your questions on the pad and we'll see if we can answer them. Then we'll see what we have left."

I went to the office and got my pad. Before I could get settled on the couch, Sally Mae asked a question, "Do you need someone to type up what you know?"

Tom and I both looked at her.

"Well, I took some secretarial classes a year ago. I was looking to get out of working in a bar. If Mike and I were going to start a new life, I wanted new skills. I can type it into a word format for you."

I turned and went after my laptop. Sally Mae might hear something I missed. I also grabbed the tape recorder. With it going, anything Sally Mae or I missed would be on tape. It took a few minutes to get everybody set up then we started.

Tom began, "Bobby James Appleton, according to what Sally Mae told us was beaten to death by Bubba who was angry at Bobby James for taking off in his prized truck. We know this from Sally Mae's statement. Who fired the shot into Bobby James' head? Why was the shot fired? We also know from an incident in Kentucky Bubba served time for beating a man in a bar room brawl. It would seem Bubba did not fire the shot into Bobby James' head?"

He went to the Mike West section of the board. "Mike knew his killer. He previously talked with Bubba then faked a fight to make it look as though Sally Mae had been kidnapped. He hid her on the Appleton farm in the bunkhouse and gave her a key so she was free to come and go. Mike met up with someone in the Appleton barn and whatever happened; Mike ended up with a broken neck and was hung from the rafters for Mrs. Appleton to find. This was not the work of Bubba. Had it been Bubba, Mike would have taken a beating and been left where he fell. Which leaves us with the questions; 1) Who did Mike trust enough for the person could get behind him and snap his neck? 2) Why did the killer make it look like a suicide? 3) Why did the killer make us want to think it was Bubba?"

I heard the clicking of the laptop keys as I wrote the big questions on my pad. I knew we were onto something. I just didn't get the why yet. It was close. I'd get it soon.

Tom was ready to do the Jeff Dunning board. He looked at both of us first to make sure we were keeping up. He started in, "Macy and I visited Jeff to find out if he had copies of the interviews in the Bobby James Appleton case. The original interviews were missing. All we had was a list of the people interviewed. Macy has already interviewed Mrs. Appleton. Mr. Appleton is deceased, having died a year after his son. We were in the process of trying to locate, Sally Mae Davis and Bubba Waxman. Macy was intending to see Mike West at the Appleton farm in the morning. Jeff gave us his case notebook. In his notebook we found notes on all the cases he and Drew Riley worked as partners. We made photo copies of the notebook and Macy secured both in a safe. Later the notebook was scanned into a computer and saved on flash drives. I have one and Macy has the other. Jeff turned up dead the next morning apparently from a suicide. From the coroner's report we know Jeff's neck had been broken much the same as Mike's. The gunshot was done postmortem—after death. Again we have questions; 1) Who did Jeff know well enough and trust enough so he was able to come up behind Jeff and he didn't feel threatened? 2) How did that same person know where Jeff kept his service revolver? 3) Why did he stage the suicide once again pointing us in the direction of Bubba?"

Tom quickly turned the board around. There he had assembled a board I knew nothing about. At the top was a paper which said, 'Drew Riley.' I smiled. We *had* been on the same page all along.

"This is the new board. It is filled with our prime suspect. Drew Riley is currently a member of the Rivers Edge Police Force. He rides patrol by choice. He's an ex-marine. His wife, Alana, left him about fifteen years ago. She took their two daughters, Alyssa and Amya. She has relocated in another state and has remarried. Riley has finished paying child support for Alyssa and has two more years to pay on Amya. Neither of the girls have seen their father since the divorce. They believe their step-father is their father. The couple has two other children both boys. I called the ex-Mrs. Riley after locating her and found out she suspected her husband of being a dirty cop. She said some young boy kept coming to the house and the last time she remembered him coming was when Bobby James went missing. She never saw him after and left her husband a year or two later. She said Riley had a mean streak. It got worse when he was drinking. There were a lot of domestic calls to the home Riley had hidden from the brass. Alana decided the only way for her was to just run. She had help from family and friends. It is my belief Riley has no idea where Alana went and I'd like to keep it that way. It is also my belief the young man who kept coming around when he was in trouble was Bubba. I think he mistakenly believed Riley was his long lost father. Which leaves us with the following questions; 1) What made Riley think reopening the Appleton case would give him problems? 2) What did he do when Bubba came to him the night of Bobby James' murder? 3) Is he the man who killed Mike and Jeff?"

"Okay, ladies, I am now open for some answers."

There was silence as Sally Mae finished typing and I stopped writing. I knew Tom and I had reached the same conclusions from different angles.

CHAPTER EIGHTEEN

Sally Mae was the first one to speak, "Bobby James and Bubba were still fighting when Mike took me home. I never heard a gunshot. I never even saw a gun. Who had a gun?"

"Good question. Who shot Bobby Appleton and why? Makes me think someone else was involved." I added it to the bottom of my list.

"If I hadn't been so upset that night, I'd have called 9-1-1 to send an ambulance out there. Of course, Mike didn't call either. We talked about that a lot."

I nodded, "One of those regrets you cannot go back and change."

"Okay," Tom said a thoughtful expression on his face, "We have one more question on our list. Maybe, just maybe Bubba didn't kill Bobby James after all."

"I remember Mike saying Bubba being in town was going to stir up a hornet's nest. It's why we were going to leave town this weekend. As soon as he got his check he was going to cash it and clean out his bank account. Then we were going to get my money and head southwest."

"Well, Mike was right. We have our hornet's nest, but I'm wondering if Bubba might also be in someone's way," Tom commented.

"Do we need to get him a message? I don't want anyone else to die," Sally Mae said with a look of concern.

"I think it's being taken care of, but he could still be in danger," I replied.

"You know, come to think of it, Officer Riley seems to be always hanging around. He tried to hit on me at one time. When it didn't work he seemed to be everywhere. He would pull me over for no reason. He did the same thing to Mike. He even stopped by where I was doing hair, kinda like he was checking up on me. Letting me know he could find me. It was creepy." She shuddered at the memory.

"Thanks for the input, Sally Mae. We need to move on to our other questions," Tom said abruptly.

I thought it was odd Tom had cut her off, but I was sure he was trying to get to something.

"Mike West who did he trust? Who would not pose a threat to him? Why did his death have to look like a suicide?" Tom went on.

"He would have trusted a police officer. Which one? Why with Bubba in town was he not a bit on edge, he was talking to an officer?" I kept hammering out my questions without waiting for an answer.

Tom held up his hand. "You might be on to something, Macy. Sally Mae, were there any police officers Mike was friendly with?"

"No one who comes to mind, he knew most of them since he grew up here. Mike wasn't one to get in trouble with the law," she stated, but she seemed to be considering the question.

"It's true. He didn't even have a parking ticket. So, we know he might have been with a police officer. We need to find out which one," Tom said running his hands through his hair. It was a sign he was getting frustrated.

"Do we have IA files coming today?" I asked hoping to get our focus back.

"We have them coming but only on the two officers involved in the Bobby Appleton case," he replied curtly.

"It's a good start," I said even though I was getting frustrated with Tom.

"May I ask what IA is?" Sally Mae wanted to know.

"It's internal affairs. They keep files on all of us," I told her hoping she wouldn't ask why they kept them.

"Okay, thanks." She seemed satisfied with my answer.

"Can we look at the Jeff Dunning questions?" Tom asked as he paced.

"They are pretty much just the same as Mike's. Who would Jeff have trusted? A fellow officer would be logical. Who would know where he kept his weapon? It would be someone who visited him often."

"You're right, Macy. He left us in his living room when he went to his basement office. It could have been anyone," Tom was finding it hard to question a fellow officer. These were men he had worked with for years.

"If you look at the Drew Riley questions, do you wonder if Bubba thought Riley was his father?" I asked trying to come at things from a different angle.

"Good question." Tom stopped and looked at me.

"Wait." We both looked at Sally Mae. "Bubba used the extra garage at Riley's. It's where he fixed up his truck. I'll bet Riley even helped him."

"How do you know?" I asked.

"We hung out there sometimes. Bubba would sneak beer to us from Riley's fridge," she said with animation.

"Did Riley ever come hang out with you?" It seemed like Tom thought we might be onto something.

"Sometimes when he was home, he'd come out if he thought it was getting late. He'd send us home and tell us he'd better find us in school the next morning. We'd leave and he and Bubba would stand there and watch us."

"Is it possible that Bubba could have been staying with Riley?" I was curious about this development myself.

"It would explain why there was a cot and chest in a restricted area. I always thought maybe Riley had girls out there. Or he stayed there when his wife was mad at him."

"It's something to look into." Tom suggested.

"Does anyone else think Bubba mistook Riley for his father?" I tossed that question out to see what it would bring in.

Sally Mae looked puzzled and Tom's facial expression revealed the question had caught him totally off guard. Silence told me they were thinking now it could be a possibility.

Finally Tom spoke, "It would explain why Jeff continued to send money to Bubba's mom. He didn't know Bubba was his son."

"So, how did he convince Riley, he was his son?" I was perplexed.

"Maybe he didn't have to. Maybe Riley knew about Dunning's son and just played along. Maybe he thought he could use the information at some point in the future. Remember Dunning had put Bubba on his insurance," Tom reminded me.

"What could he use it for?" Sally Mae asked innocently.

"Which brings me to this," Tom said as he turned the second board over. On it was the banking information I found on Drew Riley and he added banking information on Jeff Dunning. "It seems the men had a second income. Riley's was more than Dunning's. Dunning's alone would not have drawn any suspicion. Riley's might have made someone look twice if they were looking at all. Riley tends to live large. I've also learned Dunning left his house and money to Angela Waxman. She doesn't know it yet. It should make her life more comfortable."

"If Bubba knew, would it make him a suspect? He might have killed his father so his mother could live better?" Sally Mae asked her face pinched in puzzlement.

"Sally Mae, it might be true if Bubba truly cared about his mother. She is just another woman to wait on him. He's never done anything to make her life easier," Tom was disgusted with the way Bubba had treated his mother.

Sally Mae shook her head in disbelief. Some of this was turning her world upside down. Yet I think she secretly had suspected part of it for a long time.

"So, where are we going from here? First, we know that both, Mike and Jeff trusted someone who could get close enough to kill them without causing either man to even fear for his life. We also know Dunning and Riley were part of an activity other than police work which brought them extra money. Lastly, someone is out there killing anyone connected to the Appleton case. What we don't know is who?" I stated clarifying our discussion.

Tom answered quietly, "We both have suspicions. I've contacted the captain. He's putting Riley under surveillance and he's going to warn Bubba personally to watch his back. He's taken this so seriously he's going to take my wife and boys to her parents which is sixty miles away."

"Are we still safe here?" Sally Mae asked fear creeping into her voice.

"We think so. As far as we know, only Mrs. Appleton and the captain know where we are. Since Mike has so much stored in the bunker, we don't have to worry about food. We might get bored with the variety, but we have food. None of us are going out in the daylight hours or at night unless it's to meet with the captain. We're going to get very tired of each other. There won't be any going outside during the day to stretch our legs. Also we'll pull the blackout shades before we turn on lights at night. Too bad we didn't think to pack board games." Tom told us.

Sally Mae laughed. "There are board games in the hall closet. Mike thought of everything."

We all laughed as the tension in the room broke.

CHAPTER NINETEEN

Sally got up and headed for the kitchen. As usual she was think-ing of our stomachs, so she got underway making dinner. I had no idea what she would come up with tonight, but I knew from past experience it would be wonderful. She hummed off key while she worked.

Tom and I took our boards down for the moment. We put each person's information in a folder. Bobby James was fuller than when we started. Mike and Jeff's were about the same. The new file on Drew Riley was just getting started. If Riley was our killer, I won-dered how long it would be before he did some serious looking for us. I could see myself getting cabin fever very soon.

Tom took everything to our office and I took my laptop back to my room. We were going to have to count on the captain to be our only back up and he didn't know all we did. This was one of those times when I wished my dad were still alive; he'd know what to do.

I heard the TV turn on, so I picked up my yarn and headed toward the living room. Sally Mae was curled up watching *Wheel of Fortune.* I knew the gist of the game and watched. I laughed when Sally Mae and I found ourselves trying to solve the puzzles. We took turns guessing as if we were the contestants. The show was heading to the bonus round when Tom joined us. The bonus round consisted of two words. In the first were two blanks, an L, two blanks, and an

E. The second word had five blanks, an E, and an R. Tom took one look and said, "Police Officer."

"No way," I said incredulously.

The contestant chose a C, M, D and an O. They filled in the letters and started the timer. Two C's and two O's showed up in the puzzle. Sally Mae and I both looked at Tom. He laughed.

"Shannon and I take each other on every night. She wins more often than I do." He shrugged.

The timer ran out and they showed the puzzle. Sure enough "Police Officer" was what they were looking for.

"Since we now know who the puzzle solver is, I'm going to check on dinner. You can watch something else if you want." Sally Mae headed to the kitchen after handing the remote to Tom.

"So what's up next?" Tom asked.

"Got me, I don't spend much time watching TV." I had one but rarely turned it on. Those times when I did it was often just for background noise since I rarely sat to watch a program.

Tom picked up the remote and started channel surfing. After scrolling through several he settled on of all things a police drama.

I went to work on my afghan and tantalizing smells drifted in from the kitchen. All was well at the moment.

Sally Mae started setting the table and I took my yarn back to the bedroom. Tom asked if there was anything he could do to help.

"Just find your way to the table," Sally Mae said as she dished out the steaming food which smelled like chicken soup. I came back and handed Tom the first plate. I took mine from Sally Mae and headed toward the table. She brought her plate and the coffee pot. "Tea is coming, Macy."

"Thanks."

Dinner was a type of potpie concoction. Sally Mae had taken all the leftovers and mixed them together. Then she baked them in a deep-dish pan with bread on both the top and bottom. It was delicious.

After dinner, I cleaned up and Sally Mae went to watch TV. Tom had been very quiet most of the afternoon. He'd been in the office or watching TV.

"I know I said no one was leaving, so I need to know right now what you girls think you'll need to hunker down here for the long haul."

"Tom we have tons of food, why would you want to risk going out?" I asked startled at the thought.

"I'm meeting the captain in a couple of hours. Then I'll see about picking up some more supplies for you."

"Not anyplace in Rivers Edge I hope." I said sternly.

"No, we're driving north. He knows a little out of the way diner. We'll meet there."

Sally Mae piped up, "I could use a few more books and maybe a crossword or two."

"Any particular authors?" Tom asked ready to write down the names.

"I like Nora Roberts, Fern Michaels, Patricia Cornwell, and James Patterson. Basically anything that looks dangerous," she replied with enthusiasm.

"I'll let the captain know. He's doing the shopping. Macy, you have enough yarn?"

"I sure do, unless you're thinking this is going to be more than a few weeks." I answered.

"Okay, I'll call him. We'll get what you need. Then I'm going to get a message ready for my wife. I hate leaving her like this with the baby due an all," this weighed heavy on Tom. His expression was worried.

"Just in case, I'm putting in a request for baby yarn, pink, blue and white. I'll make something for the baby," I said hoping it would help ease his tension.

"You got it." He walked toward his room reaching into his pocket for his cell phone.

"Do you think it's a good idea for him to go out?" Sally Mae wanted to know.

I thought about it for a moment then said, "I'm not sure it's a good idea for anyone to go out, however, no one knows where we are right now and I'd like it to stay that way. We also need the files the captain has to build an airtight case against Riley. It has to tie him to the murders of Jeff Dunning and Mike West. Hopefully, we can figure out how to tie him to Bobby James. I want this man to go away for a long time, with no chance of parole, or getting out early for good behavior. We can't do it without some contact outside these walls."

"I guess you're right. It seemed like an adventure at first. Now it seems more frightening," was her anxious response. "I should've taken this so much more seriously years ago."

"I'd like to tell you it's going to get better, but even I don't know when it will be."

We sat quietly for a long while. Tom entered in his black jeans, black T-shirt, and black leather jacket. He turned off all the lights in the kitchen area. "Be sure to lock this when I leave. I have the key Sally Mae used, so I can let myself back in. If all goes well, I should be back in two hours."

I followed him to the door and locked it as soon as he had slipped out. It was a challenge to curb my desire to follow him in case he ran into trouble. After all, it was my job was to keep Sally Mae safe from harm.

Sally Mae settled in to watch a show called *Survivor*. I guess it had been on several weeks. It was some kind of reality show where two tribes competed against each other to see who could last the longest, become the sole survivor, and win a million dollars. Tonight's show had them spinning a wheel to see what kind of insect or other disgusting food they would have to eat. I didn't understand how or why people would put themselves through this kind of ordeal. I could tell from Sally Mae's reaction this was a show people enjoyed. Living vicariously through the participants must have been the appeal. Maybe they thought it would be cool to go live in some exotic place and battle the elements. Here, however, it seemed their teammates were also something to contend with. The whole tribal council thing gave me a new look at the lives of people. It was one I could have done without so I returned to my crochet.

Sally Mae and I spent the evening watching TV, reading, or me crocheting. We were both concerned about Tom's whereabouts. At one point Sally Mae made us both a cup of tea. Later, she made us both cocoa. We didn't really watch the clock, but we were both aware it was at least three hours since Tom had left. I was hoping he was just being cautious. I had no idea what Sally Mae might be thinking.

Finally she turned off the TV and said, "I'm going to read a little while in bed. You'll let me know if Tom comes back with some important news right?"

"Sure. Will you leave the door open so I have a light to follow when I come to bed?"

"No problem." She picked up the cups and took them to the kitchen, then headed down the hallway to what had become our room. I heard her in the bathroom. Then there was silence.

I was careful not to let Sally Mae know just how worried I was. I even considered turning off the lights and making a circuit outside the bunkhouse, but knew it wouldn't be a good idea if we were compromised. Pacing was out of the question so I didn't pace. Instead when my stress level rose high I crocheted. The afghan I had started a couple days ago was getting close to completion. I didn't know who would be the recipient of this one, but it would be ready when the time came.

The atmosphere was peaceful for about fifteen minutes, then I thought I heard something outside. Not wanting to panic, I turned off the light and headed quietly down the hallway.

When I entered our room, Sally Mae looked up; I put my finger to my lips indicating she should be quiet and she nodded. As I reached for the gun at my ankle, I asked, "Can you shoot?"

She nodded yes. I handed her the gun and pointed to the floor. I wanted her to be ready to go to the underground hideout. She quickly opened the trapdoor. I doused the light handing her one of the flashlights we kept in the room.

"I'm going back to the living room. If you hear gunfire or voices which aren't mine or Tom's, get yourself downstairs. I'll call out when I come down so you won't be shooting me. If anyone else comes down this set of stairs, shoot first and get out of there. You know where the exit is. My car is under the brush next to the grate. Take my keys and get yourself to the police station. Make them lock you in a cell and don't talk to anyone except the captain. If something has happened to him demand the State Police come. Do you understand?"

"I do." She pushed back the rug to prepare in case she needed to escape.

Then quietly keeping to the shadows, I made my way back down the hall to the living room. Once I saw the room was clear, I made my way to the kitchen. Tom would come through the kitchen door using a key. Anyone else I would shoot first and ask questions later since the cupboards would give me some protection. Time seemed to crawl as I waited. I hoped Sally Mae was safe. The bear had been a drill, this was the real thing. I could hear someone walking around outside and it definitely wasn't a bear because it had a more deliberate pace. It walked and then seemed to stop and listen. There was no mistaking the fact someone was outside. I didn't know if it was friend or foe and I wasn't taking chances.

I heard the key in the lock. Hoping it was Tom, I got my flashlight ready so I could blind the person coming in then decide if my weapon was necessary. In the meantime, I waited. Whoever was at the door also hesitated, too like it was a stand-off.

When the door swung open, I hit my flashlight and saw the gun in his hand. "Drop your weapon this is the police," I shouted.

"Macy, it's me Tom." He flipped on the kitchen light and shut the door. "What on earth is going on? Where is Sally Mae?" he shouted like a madman.

"I heard someone outside at the front of the bunkhouse. Sally Mae is in the bedroom. I'll go and get her." I said as my heartbeat started slowing.

I shut off my flashlight and holstered my weapon. Quickly I made my way to the back bedroom, "Sally Mae, it was Tom," I said somewhat breathlessly, confused when I didn't hear anything. I slowly unholstered my weapon and called, "Tom."

Tom came running down the hallway. I opened the trap door and hollered down into the room, "Sally Mae, it's me, Macy. I'm coming down." Again there was no response. I wondered why she wasn't responding.

"Go slowly, Macy, I'm going to the other entrance." Tom was gone before he finished giving me directions.

I took my flashlight and held it in my other hand. I was either going to shoot someone or blind them. All the time I wondered what had happened to Sally Mae. We'd put the dead bolt on the door so no one could get in. I hadn't heard my car, so I knew she hadn't driven off. What was going on? As I reached the bottom of the stairs, I heard the toilet flush. What?

Sally Mae stepped out of the bathroom and was startled by the sight of me weapon out. "Macy, is it clear? I didn't hear you call me."

I laughed nervously. "We better open the back door and let Tom in."

Sally Mae threw the dead bolt and opened the door. There stood Tom and Bubba. Bubba was in handcuffs. Sally Mae let out a screech. I looked up immediately not sure what to expect.

Tom nudged Bubba through the door. "Look who I found?" Tom said matter-of-factly.

"I say this is an unexpected surprise," I said stating the obvious.

Sally Mae recovered enough to say, "Bubba."

Tom taking in the situation said, "Let's all go upstairs we have a lot to discuss."

Sally Mae bolted the door. I led the way up the stairs. We all made our way to the living room. Sally Mae went to the kitchen and put on a pot of coffee on. She also put on the tea kettle for me. I had a feeling we were all going to need more than coffee, but it was a good place to start.

Tom seated Bubba at the table. "Are you going to behave, big guy or does Macy need to keep a gun on you?"

"I'll stay put," Bubba replied grudgingly his expression wary.

It made me feel better Bubba wasn't going to pose a threat. Tom removed the handcuffs and went to the office. When he came back, Sally Mae and I were serving coffee and Tom was holding the tape recorder.

"Bubba, we need to ask you some questions and we'd like to record the conversation," Tom stated. His serious expression really not giving him much choice.

"Sure I haven't done anything yet. You know, Tom, it was a good one pretending to be my friend at the bar," Bubba said as though he were trying to figure this situation out.

"Actually, I might just be saving your life," Tom replied in all seriousness.

"How so?" he asked curiously.

"Did you know Mike West and Jeff Dunning were murdered?" Tom asked.

"No way, you aren't pinning those on me," he started to stand then stopped. "I done my time for the murder I did," anger and edged his voice as he clenched his fists.

Tom looked at Sally Mae and said, "We asked you to tell the story of Bobby James' murder, now I want to get Bubba's version. Please don't interrupt. Macy, give Sally Mae your pad and let her write any questions or comments she has on it."

I scurried to get the pad and a pen. When I returned, we were ready to start. Tom took the lead on this interview.

"Bubba, I want you to tell us everything leading up to the murder of Bobby James."

"Yeah, sure, it's been long enough." He started slowly remembering the day so long ago. "Bobby James and me was going to the militia campground. Bobby wanted to know what the militia was like. I'd been to a couple of camps so I knew he wouldn't fit in. For some reason, he thought it was all glamorous or something. When I picked him up after work that night, he said he changed his mind. He was going to go find Sally Mae. He had a ring for her in his pocket. Evidently, he went to the jeweler's at lunch time and picked it out."

Sally Mae stifled a gasp.

Bubba continued, "I tried to talk him out of it. I told him she was a tramp and was running around with Mike behind his back. I even offered to take him to the bar and prove it. I had no idea Mike would be there. I didn't expect him to be dancing with her. I'd never seen Bobby James lose his temper. I didn't even know he had one. He was going to tear Mike apart right there in the bar. I told him to go outside and cool off. The jerk took off in my truck. No one drove my truck but me. I'd worked hard to restore it and it was all I had. Sally Mae seemed to know where he would go, so we piled into Mike's car and went after him. Mike and Sally Mae led the way to the tree stand. I guess Mike and Bobby James had hunted there and Sally Mae and Bobby James used it for a making out. When I finally got there Mike and Bobby James were going at it. Sally Mae was trying to squeeze herself between them and she was screaming like a banshee.

I grabbed Mike and walked him away. I thought Sally Mae would be safe with Bobby James, then she screamed and I turned Bobby James had thrown her to the ground. I didn't know what he was going to do, but I knew I'd started it and I needed to end it. I told Mike to get Sally Mae and get out of there, grabbed Bobby James, and held him while they left. When they were gone I let him go, he was still raging. I tried to calm him down. I told him I'd lied and if he wanted to fight someone, he should be fighting me. He came at me and I let him for a while. Then I started swinging back. I hit him a couple times and it's like he became a maniac again. I gave him a good shot and he fell. He hit his head on a rock and didn't get up. I felt blood and panicked.

I went to see Drew Riley. I told him my dad was going to kill me. He'd been telling me if I kept getting into trouble he was going to toss me out. Drew said not to worry he'd take care of it. I went to the garage, took a shower and went to bed.

I didn't think no more about it until everyone started looking for Bobby James on Monday afternoon. I thought Drew took him to the hospital. I was sure it was where they'd find him. I knew I was going to have to face the music this time. It was almost two more weeks before they found his body. I was sure they were going to think I done it. I was the last person seen with him. I didn't stay for his funeral. I packed my stuff and headed to my ma's. I told her everything that happened and she sent me off to Kentucky to my uncle's. I got into a scrape there about six years ago. I did my time. I ain't done nothing illegal since I got out. I came to see Mike and tell him I was sorry. It's when he told me they was looking into Bobby James' murder again. I told him I'd like to see Sally Mae and apologize, but I didn't know where she was. Next thing I know, I'm reading about Mike hanging himself in the paper. I decided to lay low. First time I come out in public I meet Tom here," he seemed resigned to the fact he was being blamed. His facial expression was one of regret.

"So, what brought you here tonight?" Tom inquired.

"When we were kids, Bobby James was trying to fix this old bunkhouse up. He thought maybe he could rent it from his folks. We used to sneak in the old tunnel when we were drinking. We'd slip out the same way in the morning. I thought maybe I could hide out here until this whole thing blew over. I was pretty surprised to find that nice Camaro out there blocking the entrance. It made getting in hard. Then the door was bolted and Tom here caught me trying to find my way back out. We tussled and he cuffed me. So, here we are," he said his shoulders slumping in resignation.

Tom flipped the tape in the recorder and looked at Sally Mae, "Do you have any questions for Bubba?"

"Why?" she sobbed, "What did I ever do to you it? You wanted to turn Bobby James against me? What did you do with the ring?"

"I wasn't into the whole get married thing. I thought Bobby James should be his own man first. If he didn't join the militia, he could at least taste life without a woman. I had nothing against you personally. You were just another dumb chick who wanted to tie the knot and have babies. I wasn't real keen on the family scene. Mine hadn't been real great. I never saw the ring after Bobby put it back in his pocket. I figured it would be with his stuff when they found him. I really didn't know he was dead. I thought he'd crawled off somewhere to heal. I even checked here in the bunkhouse. I didn't mean for him to die." Bubba hung his head between his hands.

I felt the truth in his words. He'd not intended for anyone to die. I wasn't certain he'd killed Bobby James. "Bubba, why did you go to Drew Riley and not your father?" I asked curious.

"Jeff had told me if I screwed up one more time, he was done with me. I didn't want this stupid thing to be what ended our relationship. In the end, it did anyway," his voice carried regret and his shoulders sagged even lower.

Tom asked, "When did you find out Jeff was your father?"

"I was in eighth or ninth grade when I came across some papers Ma had said something about my dad being a cop. When I asked her about it, she said he was very distinguished at his job. I got all mad and asked what kind of respectable man left a woman to raise her child alone? Ma cried and tried to explain he hadn't known about the pregnancy when they split up and he was married to someone else. She kept talkin' but I stormed out of the house. I got quite a chip on my shoulder. I hung out around the police station in town every chance I got. I was trying to find one who might look like me. I started wearing a leather jacket and smoking to see if I could get their attention. When it didn't work, I did some petty stuff and made sure I got caught. I was sure my father would step up and take me outside to knock some sense into me. It never happened so, when I turned sixteen I quit school and came here to see what I might find. I hung out at the school looking for guys I could pal around with, guys who didn't care if my Ma worked at the diner and didn't marry my dad. It's how I met Bobby James and Mike. We took turns scoping out cops. Bobby James found a long-range camera, we took photos of the cops, and of me to use for comparison. We took black and white photos and Mike knew how to develop the pictures. Finally we saw the resemblance between me and Jeff," he said impressed with their savvy back then.

"It took a while for me to work up the nerve to talk to him. When I did, it wasn't anything like I'd planned. He was hoping someday Ma would tell me who he was. He told me about sending Ma money to help with my support. He told me I should get into night school. He'd help me, gave me a room in his house, and put me on his insurance. He told Drew about me and I met him. Drew was the kind of guy I'd hoped my dad would be. Just a little on the edge. He liked to work on cars and helped me redo the old truck. He fixed me a room in the garage so if it was late I could stay there. I didn't stay in school long, but I was having the time of my life. Drew got me smokes and beer. Dad had a fit. It was like Drew was holding something over him and I couldn't figure out what. The more Dad talked down about Drew, the more time I spent with him. They weren't good friends but they were partners and had to count on each other. It made him blow a gasket when he couldn't interview me after Bobby James turned up dead. Drew fixed it so the whole thing went away. It was one more thing to make Dad mad. I packed the truck and took off. See the family thing just didn't work for me," the long pent up frustration seemed to be coming out in his words. Bubba was a kid no one seemed to want unless he conformed to their way of thinking.

Tom stopped the tape. "It's late. Bubba can bunk in the room with me. I'll make sure we're all locked up. We can talk more in the morning."

Everyone agreed. Sally Mae and I washed the coffee mugs and spoons. Then we headed for the bedroom. Tom checked the locks and led Bubba to the other end of the bunkhouse.

As I turned off the light I was prepared for Sally Mae to start in with a million questions. I was surprised to hear a couple of sobs and then silence. She was trying to understand the things leading to the death of Bobby James, the man who really had wanted to marry her.

CHAPTER TWENTY

Yelling from the kitchen brought me awake with a start. "What do you mean I'm not free to leave? I didn't kill no one. I'm not planning to either. I just came to apologize to Mike and Sally Mae. I wanted to see how life was for them and if they were happy. I don't mean no harm to her now," Bubba was shouting furiously.

Tom's response came out in almost a hiss, "I know that. It's you I'm trying to protect. Whoever killed Mike West and Jeff Dunning is out there trying to kill Sally Mae and pin it all on you. Got any ideas who it might be, hot shot? If you don't, I've got one and I'm not even sure if I can bring him in. Are you ready to die?"

I slipped on my robe and pulled the bedroom door closed behind me. Sally Mae didn't need to hear this. She had a rough night. I heard her sobbing off and on during the night. While I wanted to offer comfort, I wasn't sure it would be welcomed. I thought maybe we'd get a chance to talk in the morning. Now with the guys going at it, it didn't seem like a possibility.

I spoke the minute I hit the living room. "Do you think you two numbskulls can put your testosterone in check? It's not necessary to wake everyone in the county is it?"

They both turned at once. I must have looked a fright standing there with my hair wild and my robe belted around my nightshirt.

After a full two minutes of silence I said, "Much better. Sally Mae cried most of the night. I think it was over the things she's lost starting with Bobby James. She didn't sleep well, so I didn't sleep well. Are you really looking forward to spending the day with two grumpy females? I'm heading back to make myself look presentable and I better find the two of you cooking a wonderful breakfast. I don't need to see you liking each other, but I better not hear any more raised voices. Are there any questions?"

Seeing neither of them begin to talk, I turned and left the room. It took a minute, but I started hearing the sounds of breakfast being started. It would give them a cool down to know there were others also at risk.

Sally Mae was sitting up in her bed when I opened the door grinning from ear to ear. "I don't know what I missed, but you sure gave it to them. I'm sorry; I didn't mean to keep you up."

"It's fine. I just didn't know if you wanted to talk about it or just needed to get it out of your system. I thought maybe if you wanted we could talk this morning. Before those two started in on each other."

"I heard them yelling but I was back at the fight with Bobby James and Bubba in my dream. I thought the voices were just a part of the dream. When I heard you light into them I realized it was morning."

"Let's get ready to face the day. I'm afraid one of us is going to have to referee today. Sure you don't want the job?" I asked my voice dripping with sarcasm.

Sally Mae laughed and shook her head from side to side, "Not me."

We both dressed quickly and headed toward the kitchen. To my surprise, Tom was at the stove with bacon frying in one pan and a skillet just about ready for pancakes. Bubba had taken out dishes and was setting the table. The coffee was almost ready and water was on to boil for my tea. This is the way mornings should be.

Sally Mae moved to the couch and picked up the remote. She surfed until she found a morning news show. It was just about to start when they were interrupted by an important news message. We all stopped what we were doing to hear what had gone wrong in the world now.

"This just in, police Captain Buzz Wellington was shot outside his home last night. It is this reporter's understanding Captain Wellington had been at a late staff meeting and was returning home. The extent of his injuries is unknown at this time. We will keep you updated…in other news…"

Sally Mae hit the mute button, the silence in the room was deafening. We all looked at each other. It was Tom who broke the silence.

"You might as well turn it back on. We are going to need a good breakfast to get to the bottom of this and we'll need to hear updates."

The guys returned to what they were doing. Sally Mae unmuted the TV and then turned it down. We were stunned and did not know how this would affect our situation. Breakfast was a somber affair. Sally Mae started the dishes as soon as we were through.

"Okay, do you want to let me in on what's going on?" Bubba finally asked his early morning frustration still in his voice.

I filled the coffee cups for Tom and Bubba; I put the kettle on for another cup of tea and said, "Sit here. Tom and I will try to fill you in on what we know."

Tom sipped his coffee then started, "We think Riley had a go at Bobby James and killed him with a shot between the eyes also he wanted people to believe you or the militia had killed him. When you came back into town, Mike panicked. He staged a shouting match at Sally Mae's apartment and brought her here. I don't know if Mike thought you'd hurt her or if you'd make things worse for him. He was planning to leave on Friday with her. They were going to get married and start a new life. If you told Sally Mae about the ring, she might not have gone with him. The same afternoon Macy interviewed Mrs. Appleton, Mike came out to do some last minute chores and someone found him in the barn. Whoever it was, was someone Mike had no reason to distrust. The person got behind him, broke his neck, and then he strung him up from the rafters to make it look like a suicide. The next day, Macy and I paid a visit to Jeff, because all of the interviews done when Bobby James disappeared and later was found dead were missing. We wanted to know if Jeff had kept copies. Instead, he gave us a notebook he kept. It had several cases in it and some stuff we thought was a little off. The next morning Jeff was found in his living room. Apparently he had committed suicide with his service revolver. The ME (medical examiner) found that Jeff's neck had been snapped. Which meant someone else used his weapon to stage a suicide."

Tom took a moment to let the information sink in and took a drink of his coffee. Bubba looked like he had just walked into a horror show.

I broke the silence saying, "Captain Wellington thought he needed Tom and me in protective custody, but he didn't feel we'd be safe at work. He told us to find some place to hole up and to call him only on his cell phone. We came to see if we could use a barn not in use and Mrs. Appleton told us Mike had fixed up the bunkhouse and there was cable TV and something called WIFI. We hid my Camaro and the rental. While we were checking the place out Sally Mae let herself in the back door with a key Mike had given her. She was shocked to see us and more shocked to learn Mike would not be coming for dinner. She told us pretty much what you did about the night Bobby James went missing and later turned up dead. We had you as our prime suspect, thought you might have killed Mike, were looking to kill Sally Mae, and clean up loose ends so to speak. We traced your life then Tom went to see your mother. Which made you our first suspect in the Jeff Dunning murder. Tom meeting you in the bar was no accident. He had the captain in a car outside. Tom followed you to where you were staying and the captain kept watch on you all night. We got your prison record from Kentucky and learned you killed a man in a bar fight. So sneaking up on someone and snapping their neck did not go along with what we knew about you. We started looking into who else might have been involved in the Appleton investigation and came up with Drew Riley. We wondered if you thought Riley was your father and it's why you hung out with him. The more we looked at Riley the more he became a suspect and you were in danger. Tom met with the captain last night. He gave us some files we need to go over, but without covering his own tracks. Does Riley know you are in town?"

Bubba gave a negative shake of his head, still trying to process everything we told him. Finally he said, "I haven't been to Drew's yet. So, I don't know if he knows I'm here or not. Does that make me a target?"

Tom took a deep breath, "Yes, we think you are also a target. What I am hoping is, he was too busy following the captain last night he didn't have time to follow me. I need to go out and hide my car as well as throw cover over the underground opening. You want to take a chance and come with me? It might be the last time you get outside for a while."

Bubba pushed back his chair and said, "Count me in. I'd like to be one of the good guys for a change."

Together the men went out the back door and Tom led the way toward the lean-to. I looked at Sally Mae and asked, "Do you think he knows anything else?"

"He might know if Drew Riley was taking bribes or something. About the murders, I don't think he has a clue. Right now I would think he is as scared as I am," her reply was an honest assessment of her feelings.

"For right now, I believe we're safe. I just don't know for how long," I told her raking my own hands through my hair.

CHAPTER TWENTY-ONE

They came in laughing, but I doubted they'd become fast friends. Sally Mae was curled up with a book on one end of the couch and I was on the other working on the afghan.

"Doesn't this look homey?" Bubba asked taking in the scene.

"Don't let appearances deceive you; Macy has her weapon under all the yarn. Sally Mae is pretending to read. My guess is she hasn't turned a page in the twenty minutes we've been gone," Tom said chuckling.

Sally Mae smiled sweetly and said, "I'd take that bet, Bubba. I've read an entire chapter since you two left."

Bubba snickered and relaxed a bit. "What are we going to do?"

"Well, the captain dropped off a couple files Macy and I need to go through. While we're working you and Sally Mae could get reacquainted. I would just ask you not try to leave the bunkhouse."

"I'll go get the files and we can work at the table, then we can keep an eye on Sally Mae and Bubba. Someone might need to referee," I suggested as I got up.

Sally Mae let out the first real laugh I'd heard from her. "Macy, you're a hoot. I think Bubba and I can manage without the two of you as chaperones. Go work your magic in the office; I'll bring coffee and tea if I think you've been in there too long."

Tom and I headed for the office. I took Jeff's IA file and Tom took Riley's. I grabbed my pad and a pen to make notes as I read and Tom did the same.

Sally Mae came in at some point and set a cup of tea next to me and a cup of coffee next to Tom. She said nothing and left quietly.

I continued to read and make notes. When I finished I looked at Tom. He was reading the last page so I waited.

"I smell good things coming from the kitchen," Tom said when he finished. "Shall we eat and then share what we know with our friends?"

"If you don't want to discuss it first, it's fine with me." I picked up both our cups and followed Tom to the kitchen.

"Well, well, we don't have to eat alone after all," Bubba commented as we came into the room.

"I told you the smell of food would bring them out." Sally Mae gave an I-told-you-so smile.

Tom took his cup and filled it with coffee. The table was already set so he went to it and sat down. Sally Mae took my cup and added a tea bag and water. Then she handed it back to me. I too made my way to the table. In a few short minutes, Sally Mae had lunch ready. She brought it to the table and we all dug in. There was little conversation. Tom and I were still processing what we read and Sally Mae and Bubba were trying to contain their questions. Once lunch was over it was going to be a free for all, questions, comments, more questions, and hopefully a workable plan.

I helped Sally Mae clear the table and do the dishes. Tom went to the office grabbed the two files and pads with our notes. Bubba took a second cup of coffee and waited. I could he knew something was going to come out of this by the nervous bouncing of his leg. It was all he could do to stay seated.

With the dishes done and put away, Sally Mae and I joined Tom and Bubba at the table. Sally Mae gave everyone who wanted it coffee. I passed on a cup of tea.

Tom started, "As you both know, I got two files from Captain Wellington last night. They were IA files on Jeff Dunning and Drew Riley. I read Riley's and Macy read Jeff's. Since Jeff is dead, I'm going to let Macy tell you what she found or didn't find."

I took my notes and the file. "At first the file read just like most other IA files do. Just background and history of the officer's work on the job, then the tone of the file changed. There were suspicions of tampering with evidence; however they could not be proven. There were suspicions of excess income; again it could not be proven. Although Jeff had some money for which no one could account, his wife, Molly had also worked and had inherited a small sum of cash from an aunt. There was no reason to continue looking at him. Then the Appleton murder case was suddenly declared a cold case. Jeff thought there was something suspicious about it and complained to IA, but couldn't provide evidence of a cover up, so the case was shelved.

Here are my questions. Where did the excess money go? I also wondered why he was against closing the Appleton case. Did he know something we still don't?"

Tom started in before anyone could say anything. "Riley's file was also typical. He was a good officer and had a good close rate on cases. Around the time of the Appleton case, Riley's wife left him. He seemed to have more money than could be accounted for, but no one could find the source. When Bobby James was found, he was quick to say it was a rogue militia member and closed the case unsolved. He has been under suspicion for a long time, but no one has been able to find anything which could be used in prosecution.

It leaves me with these questions: One what does he really know about Bobby James murder? Two what made him cover it up? Three is he on the take somehow?"

"I can maybe help some," Bubba said quietly. "Jeff was madder than a wet hen when Bobby James' murder got closed. He didn't understand and I thought Drew got it closed trying to cover for me. It was another reason I left town. If I wasn't around, I thought people would forget." His own remorse was evident from his forlorn look.

"But the extra money wasn't from being a bad cop; at least I don't think it was," he said eagerly. "It was from taking old evidence and selling it, stuff from cases which were old and had been solved. You know old guns, drugs, and other stuff just sitting on a shelf. Stuff he could sell out of town. Jeff didn't like it, but I always felt Drew had something he held over Jeff's head to make him go along." He shrugged and I got the impression he wished he'd known his dad better.

"Oh, no, do you think it's possible Drew was the one who killed Bobby James?" Sally Mae's outburst left us all stunned. We thought of him as the killer of Mike and Jeff, but Bobby James?

"Sally Mae, what are you saying?" I asked wanting to be clear about what she was saying.

"Well, they said Bobby James had been shot in the head. Bubba and I talked about it while you were reading. Bobby James was still breathing when Bubba went to Drew for help. He thought Drew would call for an ambulance so he crashed in Drew's garage and they didn't talk about it again. Bubba came in on his own to the police station when Bobby James was found dead. He repeated for Drew everything he told him the night it happened. No one ever questioned him after the interview. It was like the case was closed, but no one went on trial."

I took a minute to process what she said. It jived with what Mrs. Appleton believed. Someone on the force knew who had killed Bobby James and closed the case to keep it quiet. I could see Tom was processing the information, too. His eyes squinted and his lips pursed in a thin line which told me the gears in his brain were turning.

"Bubba, did you and your dad ever talk about Bobby James' murder?" I asked wondering what they might have said.

"No, I never talked to Jeff before I lit out of town. I went to Ma's and she helped me get to Kentucky. If I'd been smart, I'd a made something of myself. Instead I got drunk and beat a man to death. I don't even remember what we were fighting about. I know it took three guys to pull me off him. Do you think Jeff died believing I killed Bobby James?" His frown said he regretted it.

"No, I think he believed you were innocent and which is why he gave us his notebook. I also believe it's what got him killed. He would have trusted Drew Riley and allowed him to move around in his house. I believe Drew Riley killed both Mike West and Jeff Dunning. I also think he's after you and Sally Mae," I told him honestly.

Sally Mae gave a little gasp her hand covering her mouth and her eyes wide, "I's why you've had me under lock and key? It wasn't to keep Bubba from hurting me?"

Tom raised an eyebrow at this and then said, "At first we thought it was Bubba. Then we figured out there was a second killer, one who was killing in cold blood. It was the reason I made contact with Bubba. I needed to be sure he wasn't after you. It's when Macy and I figured it had to be someone connected with the case and the only person left was Drew Riley. He is trying to connect the murders to Bobby James. He wanted to be the hero cop and bring Bubba in with enough evidence to make a circumstantial case against him and send him back to prison."

Bubba rocked the table trying to stand, "That son of a bitch! I trusted him. I didn't want Bobby James dead and I didn't ask him to kill anyone. I didn't want Mike or Jeff dead either. I came back to try to make up for the guilt I felt because I hadn't done the right thing, like go to my dad or call an ambulance." His face was red as he tried to hold his temper in check.

He was angry. We were going to have to harness his anger if we were going to get Riley without anyone else getting hurt or killed.

In a soft calm voice I said, "Bubba, sit down please. We need to pick your brain. Do you know where Riley sold the things he took from evidence? Do you remember seeing him get any pay-offs?"

Bubba threw himself into the chair. He held his head in his hands before saying anything. "I knew where he kept the stuff in the garage, but I'm not sure if he still keeps it there. I don't know who he sold the stuff to or when he got paid off. Ugh, this is so bad. I don't know why I didn't see it coming."

"You were a wild kid when it first started. No one was supposed to die. It wasn't supposed to get pinned on you. You had no idea coming back was going to lead to more murder." Sally Mae reached out and put her hand on Bubba's arm.

The gesture of comfort was not lost on him. He covered her small hand with his. "I would never hurt you. I didn't mean to hurt you all those years ago. I just didn't want Bobby James to get married and break up the threesome he, Mike, and I had formed. I also didn't understand you could have made it better for all of us."

"I know," she whispered, "I know."

"We agree we know who the murderer is. It's important we keep as low a profile as possible. I can't be sure it was Drew Riley who tried to take out the captain. I also can't rule out the possibility it was him who shot the captain. We *cannot* call the captain as we don't know what condition he's in. There is no one in the department we can trust at this time. So, we are going to get on each other's nerves and we are going to stay inside this bunkhouse until further notice. Now, Mrs. Appleton is the only person who knows we're here and she only knows about Macy and me. She likes Macy so I doubt she'd tell anyone unless she was threatened with death. I'm not even sure she'd give us up then," Tom's comments were to the point; the four of us were stuck here.

"I can't call her they may have tapped her phone. I could sneak up after dark, but I don't want to frighten her. It would make me feel better to know she is okay, though," looking at the others I for approval of that idea.

"We need to do something about her and we also need some help. I'm for contacting the State Police. This will probably be the most farfetched thing they've ever heard. I need to do some research and see who we should contact. I'm open for any and all suggestions," Tom put it out there as if we were a team.

No one said anything, finally Sally Mae broke the silence, "I think we should chance Macy going to see Mrs. Appleton. I don't want to take a chance someone would harm her. She's a nice woman who's lost everything; her son, her husband, and now Mike. Please, let Macy go see her tonight."

"If you're worried about Macy going out, Sally Mae and I will be fine here. We can even be locked in the safe room. I'm not about to let anyone in here to hurt her," Bubba suggested his eyes resting on Sally Mae.

"I'm sure we can work something out. Macy, do you want to try and see Mrs. Appleton tonight," Tom asked looking directly at me.

"I would and I agree with Sally Mae, I don't want her hurt anymore than she already has been. Besides, she needs to know that we are okay."

"It's settled then. You and I will head up to her house after dark. Sally Mae and Bubba will stay here. We'll make sure she's okay and then we'll skedaddle back here to the bunkhouse." Tom was ready for some action even if it was just checking on Mrs. Appleton.

"In the meantime, let's get this table cleaned off," Sally Mae suggested, "I'll throw some sandwich stuff on the table and we can have sandwiches for dinner. If we use paper plates there will be little clean up. You two can get ready for your evening outing. Bubba and I can hold down the fort here."

I picked up the papers and Tom took them to the office. Sally Mae got the sandwich makings out while I found paper plates and knives. Tom thought it would be a good idea to open the chips he bought. He also told Sally Mae there was a bag by the back door filled with books for her and baby yarn for me. Sally Mae took the bag back to the bedroom and then we all sat down to eat. Conversation was a bit livelier than it had been at lunch.

Bubba asked, "How did you two become partners?"

"Luck of the draw," Tom answered then added smiling, "no one else wanted her.

Next, Bubba asked Sally Mae, "So how have you been up until now?" It was two friends catching up and two others becoming friends.

"I've worked here and there, nothing for very long trying to figure out my life," she answered shyly.

Finally he got around to me, "So, Macy, how'd you end up in Rivers Edge?"

It was the question I most hated but I answered him honestly, "I'd lost my fiancé in the line of duty and needed a change."

The personal questions helped to keep our minds off the real reason we were all here.

CHAPTER TWENTY-TWO

We whiled away the hours until sunset playing Scrabble. Sally Mae and I took on the guys. Then Sally Mae and Bubba took on Tom and me. After the second game, Tom and I went to change. We both dressed in all black. I pulled my hair up into a black watch cap and Tom wore one, too. We didn't take any chances just in case someone might see us. As we approached the farmhouse, Tom whispered, "I need to take out the light or you'll be a sitting duck on the porch. I'm going in the side door there on the barn. Give me ten minutes. I need to get to the hayloft and unscrew the light. When it goes out you make your way to the porch. I'll keep watch from up there."

I nodded and crept as close to the house as I could get while still staying in the shadows. I saw Tom let himself in the barn and I waited. The night was warm and mosquitoes buzzed annoyingly around my head. I held my spot without moving. I was sweating and the bugs were making me crazy. It took a while but finally the light on the barn went out. Since that was my cue, I crept slowly to the back porch and knocked on the door. It took a few minutes, but Mrs. Appleton opened the door and I found myself pinned to the spot by a high-powered flashlight.

I hissed, "Please, Mrs. Appleton, turn off the light."

Once she realized it was me, she turned off the light and opened the door to let me in.

"I'm so sorry, Detective McVannel. Do come right in." She led the way to her kitchen preparing for our usual talk.

"Please don't turn on the light," I said. "I need to talk to you and I don't want anyone to know I'm here."

"Something bad has happened hasn't it?" Her weathered face etched with worry.

"Depends on what you call bad. Move back into your living room and I will sit on the floor in the hallway. Then we will be able to talk." I told her.

She quickly moved to her chair and turned to face me. She picked up some knitting she was working on.

I sat out of view of the windows. It would look like a normal night in the Appleton household and normal was what I was going for.

"Mike was planning to leave town and take Sally Mae with him. They were going to marry and start over. Someone thought Mike was a threat since we were looking into Bobby's case again. The person killed Mike. The same person also killed Officer Dunning. We have reason to believe, but cannot prove it yet, the person is the person responsible for killing your son."

I waited, but Mrs. Appleton said nothing. She just nodded her head. To anyone looking in from outside, she appeared to be nodding off.

I continued, "Mike had stashed Sally Mae in the bunkhouse. She's been there with us. We also have Bubba with us. He joined us the other night. Unfortunately Captain Wellington has been shot and we have no one safe to contact in the department. By the way you were absolutely right someone in the department knew who killed Bobby James and that someone is a cop. We are trying to find a safe person in the State Police to contact. In the meantime, we think you might be in danger. The officer might come to you asking for help. He could do you harm or even kill you. Would you consider coming back and staying at the bunkhouse with us?"

"You or someone with you turned out the light didn't you?" She smiled as she realized what was going on.

"Yes, Tom is in the hayloft waiting for us to come out. When we're back safely at the bunkhouse, he will turn the light back on. Then he will join us."

"You really think this person would hurt me?" she sounded very unsure of how to react.

"Most definitely, he has already killed two others covering his tracks. I wouldn't ask if I weren't concerned for your safety. We cannot be seen coming and going from here in case someone is watching the house."

"Will you tell me who it is? Who is this person who took all I had in this life and left me alone? Who is this person who took all Mrs. West had left in the world? While you are telling me who, can you also tell me why?" her voice was full of despair as she asked her questions.

"I will try to answer all your questions when I know you're safe. I can't tell you and leave you here where you could be hurt." I told her honestly.

"Give me a few minutes to throw some clothes in a bag." She stood put her knitting down and reached for the light.

"Don't turn it off yet. You may want to bring your knitting with you."

She stopped and headed toward her bedroom. It took her less than three minutes to put things in a bag. She carried a second bag which she filled with some yarn, knitting needles, and patterns. Then she turned off the light.

"I'm ready," she said firmly as if embarking on a pleasure trip.

Once our eyes adjusted to the darkness, we went to the back door. The light was still out. I slowly opened the door. Mrs. Appleton followed me out and we made sure to lock up the house. As quickly as she could move we made our way toward the back of the bunkhouse. When we were beyond the range of the light, Tom screwed it back in. He waited a few seconds to make sure nothing moved. Then he came down and made his way back to the bunkhouse where the three of us entered through the back door.

Inside Bubba and Sally Mae waited inside. They knew all of our safety hung on whether or not we had Mrs. Appleton with us. Lights flooded the kitchen as we entered.

Sally Mae had cups on the table in anticipation of a reunion. We all made our way in. I took off my watch cap and shook my head to free my hair. Tom removed his cap and ran his fingers through his hair. No one spoke. When we were seated, Sally Mae asked, "Mrs. Appleton, would you like coffee or tea?"

"Oh, my dear at this time of night could I just have a glass of cold water?"

"You got it," was Sally Mae's cheerful response.

She brought ice water for Mrs. Appleton, tea for me, and then moved to the coffee pot to get coffee for Bubba, Tom and herself. She settled herself on one side of Mrs. Appleton and Bubba was on the other side. Tom and I sat across from them. No one spoke while everyone got settled. The silence was filled with tension and anticipation.

"Mrs. Appleton, I am sorry we had to bring you here like this," Tom said by way of breaking the silence.

"It's nice to see you again. Bubba, I hear you have just returned to town. I trust things have been good for you and Sally Mae, you stopped coming to visit. I could use a good hair-do again," she greeted everyone as if it was a social gathering, which further eased the tension.

Sally Mae turned to hug the woman who should have been her mother-in-law. "I'm so glad you're okay."

"I'm fine, but I think a little too old for cloak and dagger stuff. Detective McVannel, can you tell me now, who you think might be after me?" she asked pointedly.

"It's a long story but I'll tell you the brief version. The night your son died, he and Bubba had been in a fistfight. Bubba went to get help however; whoever he went to did not provide help. We believe he killed Bobby James instead." I paused before continuing, "He is a police officer and his name is Drew Riley."

"That despicable man! I wouldn't put anything past him. He never should have become a police officer; he gives them all a bad name. You needn't have worried. I'd have never let him in my house," she said her voice full of venom.

"We have reason to believe he is very dangerous. In fact, I am worried he might be the person who shot the captain, and we have no way to verify the information."

"Oh, I can help you. The quilting circle met this morning at the church. It was all the talk. Mrs. Wellington is a part of our group, but with all that's going on; we didn't think she'd be there. Sure enough just after ten she came in. There was silence in the room until someone offered her a cup of coffee. She told us everything she knew. Here's what she shared. The captain was on his way home from a late meeting. When he pulled into his driveway, a car pulled in behind him. He walked to the car to talk to the person driving. The person pulled a gun and shot him at close range. When he fell to the ground, the car peeled out. Mrs. Wellington came running with her cell phone in her hand. She dialed 9-1-1 when she heard the shot. The captain was sitting up against the back of his car. He took the phone and told them to send an ambulance and to arrest Officer Riley." She was quite proud of being able to give us the information.

There was stunned silence in the room. It was as if time had stopped.

"Are you sure? Is the captain okay?" Tom asked still not sure he heard her clearly.

"It seems he was expecting trouble and had put on his vest before attending the meeting," she said calmly.

"I thought he looked a bit heavier, but I didn't even think he might have his vest on," Tom's face was incredulous at the thought.

"Oh, my, was he meeting here with you?" Mrs. Appleton wanted to know.

"No, Mrs. Appleton, he wasn't here. He was however, meeting with me. We wanted him to know who we thought was behind the killings. We didn't think we had enough proof. If he took a shot at the captain last night and can be identified, then they can get him for attempted murder and we can safely continue looking for evidence connecting him to Officer Dunning, Mike, and your son," the relief in Tom's voice was obvious to everyone.

"I can connect him to Bobby James. I sent him to help. I never dreamed he'd kill him," Bubba said regretfully.

Mrs. Appleton looked at Bubba, "Son, no one ever thought you killed Bobby James. We thought those militia people might have, but never you. We knew the two of you were friends."

Bubba hung his head. Mrs. Appleton patted his arm in her motherly fashion. "It's going to work out all right. You just wait and see." She turned to me, "This has been too much excitement for an old woman. Where do you want me to stay?"

"Right this way, Mrs. Appleton. We have a room just for you." I led her to the now unused room near where Sally Mae and I were sleeping.

"Thank you, Detective McVannel. I knew you'd do your best for Bobby James and me."

"You're welcome, Mrs. Appleton, but I'd really wish you would call me, Macy."

"I think we're going to be good friends, so I'll call you Macy and you call me Ida," she responded.

"I'd like that, Ida," and I knew I would like to be friends with this spritely woman.

She hugged me before I left the room. I shut the door behind me so she could have privacy and walked back to the kitchen. Sally Mae had already cleaned up the cups. The guys were sitting at the table.

"Tom, do you think we can call the captain in the morning?" I asked.

"I hope he'll call us and let us know what to do next," he said. "I'm glad to know he's not badly hurt."

"Then, I don't know about the rest of you, but I'm going to call it a day. This has been way too much excitement as Ida just told me and I agree." I felt tired from the on and off tension of the day.

CHAPTER TWENTY-THREE

When I awoke I noticed something different in the atmosphere when. I glanced over at Sally Mae, but she was still sound asleep. Wondering what time it was, I checked my cell phone for the time and saw it was early. With a strong sense of urgency, I threw on my clothes and let myself out of the room. I followed the tantalizing aroma to the kitchen and found Ida busy at work.

"Good morning, Ida, I trust you slept well," I greeted her cheerily.

She turned with a smile on her face. "I did, Macy. I can put water on for tea if you'd like. I've got the hash browns in one pan and bacon in another. I was debating whether or not I should make pancakes, too. I've got the eggs ready to scramble and there are blueberry muffins in the oven."

I chuckled in spite of myself. "Ida, you are not feeding an army. We don't need pancakes. What you have already is more than enough. Yes, I'll take a cup of tea. How can I help you?"

"Just sit and talk with me. I have the table set. I didn't know if you had assigned seats, but I've got everything on there."

"We don't have assigned seats and the table looks great," I told her.

Ida reached into the cabinet and took down a few coffee cups. Then she placed some glasses on the table for orange juice. She was in constant motion as she buzzed through the kitchen.

"What would you like to talk about this morning?" I asked, hoping she'd slow for a minute.

"Well, I was thinking. We don't know yet if Officer Riley has been arrested. So it probably isn't a good idea for any of you to leave the bunkhouse. One of my books needs to go back to the library. I could do it and make a stop at the police station, maybe try to see the captain. Or I could pay a visit to his home. If I take some of the muffins I made, I could pass information for you." I could tell she'd given this a lot of thought. It's probably what had her up so early, bustling around and baking.

"Ida, you'd make a great detective. What you told us about the captain wearing a vest was a huge relief to all of us. Let's just wait and see if he calls Tom this morning. They have had good communication while we've been here," I told her adding, "I think it's great you thought of all this."

"Okay, but I'm going to bake something else. Poor Bubba looks like he hasn't had a good meal in months," she said with genuine concern in her voice.

"I think Sally Mae thought the same thing. She's been cooking up a storm since he got here."

"Well, that girl looks a bit pale too. She was always a good girl I wonder why she never settled down," Ida wondered aloud.

"I think she and Mike were planning to. Now she may find herself caring for Bubba. We'll just have to see."

"Sally Mae and Bubba," she whispered then her face lit up with a smile. "It will work out you just wait and see."

The tea kettle started to whistle. Ida went to turn it off and poured the water over the tea bag in my cup. "Do you need cream or sugar, dear?"

"Just some cream will be fine."

She brought a small pitcher of cream with her when she brought my tea. Then she returned to her cooking. By this time, the smell of food had brought Tom out of his room followed by Bubba. It wouldn't be long until and Sally Mae joined us.

"You know, I think it's time I start using my given name. It might give me a better shot at a better life," Bubba said out of the blue.

"So, we are now going to call you Jeff?" Tom asked.

"No, I think I should be Joe. Use my middle name or Jeffery Joe. I don't want to be confused with my dad. He was a good man. I think he did something Drew Riley held over him until he killed him," he said thoughtfully.

Sally Mae had entered the room while Bubba was talking. "I think maybe you should go by JJ. It's still a nickname, but it represents both your first and middle name."

"JJ. That has a nice sound to it. I'll think about it," he smiled at her considering it.

Sally Mae smiled and found herself a place at the table. Ida started heaping food on all our plates. When she deemed them full enough, she put some on a plate for herself. We all sat down to a family breakfast at least it felt like family to me. As mismatched as we might be, we were becoming a family of sorts, or at least friends.

"What are you looking to do with your life, Bubba, I mean JJ?" Ida asked as we ate.

"First, I need to find myself a job and a real place to live, not that dump I'm in now. Then I'll see where life takes me," he answered between bites of food.

"I might be able to help with the job and the place to live. I'm short a farm hand. I could pay double what I paid Mike. He was only part-time. No one uses the bunkhouse, well generally no one uses the bunkhouse," Ida told him smiling at all of us.

"Great, Mrs. A. I'm going to start as soon as we have this Drew Riley mess cleared up," he sounded like a kid who just had his Christmas wish granted.

"Well, now we have it settled. What other problems can we solve?" she asked.

"I have something to add to Bub… JJ's day. His dad left all his worldly goods and money to your mom. You can move her to Rivers Edge and she won't need to work anymore. You can fix up your grandfather's house and sell it," Tom added.

"Wow, JJ, you've become a man of property overnight. What are you going to do with yourself?" Sally Mae was brimming with enthusiasm.

I couldn't contain myself, "Sally Mae, we were able to find out what Mike had in his will. He left his house to you and his money to be split between you and his mother."

"Mike did *that*, for me?" there was a catch in her throat in spite of her joy.

"It feels like Christmas and it's only July." Ida smiled at everyone. "I think I'll bake something really special today."

"Let's not get ahead of ourselves. We still have to solve the Drew Riley situation. We know he can be charged with attempted murder. It will carry a harsher penalty because the person he attempted to kill was the captain. We don't know yet if he's been apprehended."

I looked at Tom, "Way to kill the moment, Maxwell. Speaking of moments, how is Shannon holding up? Isn't the new baby due soon?"

Tom picked up and answered, "Shannon is fine. The boys want to know when my spy job is going to be over. They are driving her nuts. The captain put someone outside the house 24/7. He didn't want to take any chances. She also has an officer inside; I think Lynn Shorter got the job. The boys are wound up."

"Children are such a delight. When this is over, I hope you will bring them by. I'd love to meet them," Ida told him.

"Mrs. Appleton, I will be happy to. Kids should know where their food really comes from," Tom said grinning.

Breakfast continued in this light-hearted manner. Then Tom's cell phone rang and he excused himself to take the call. Sally Mae and I cleaned up the table insisting to Ida we had an arrangement; the person who cooked didn't have to clean. Bubba or JJ, as we were trying to get used to calling him, turned on the TV and a news show was on. He kept the sound low so it wouldn't disrupt our conversation. I could see he was getting antsy since we were cooped up in the bunkhouse. He needed to be doing something constructive. I was trying to think of something when Tom came back into the room.

JJ muted the TV as Tom began to talk, "The captain was on the phone, He is home and doing well. Unfortunately, Drew Riley is still on the loose. They have called in the State Police to help search for him. Macy, you and I are going to have to put all we know in report form and e-mail it to the captain. He's going to present it to a task force this afternoon. We are stuck here until further notice. So unless you have suggestions, we need to find a card table for a puzzle and board games to keep us occupied. I am open to suggestions. In the meantime, Macy, can I tear you away so we can get started?"

I was shooed out of the kitchen and into the makeshift office to prepare reports for the captain. JJ went back to the TV and Ida and Sally Mae finished the dishes. I don't know how long we'd worked when Sally Mae showed up at the door with coffee and tea.

"I don't want to interrupt, but Ida says lunch is in half an hour. Hope you two are almost finished," Then she left.

"Wow, have we been here *that* long?" Tom rubbed his neck as he asked.

I looked up from my report. "I'm almost finished. Do you want me to e-mail it to you so you can proof it and add your signature?"

"Nope, I think they are going to be pretty close. If the captain has a report from each of us with the same information he'll be able to make a presentation. His secretary can cut and paste from the two of them for him." He took a gulp of coffee and went back to his typing.

It took about five minutes for me to finish mine and hit the send button. I quickly skimmed my private e-mails. The only one I needed to answer was one from my brother. He was concerned about not hearing from me. I sent a message saying I was under-cover and would contact him soon and he should count on me for Katie's graduation. I closed down my computer and took my cup to the kitchen.

"Tom should be right behind me. He was just hitting the send button when I left," I told Ida.

"Good because lunch is ready. Have a seat. I'll get you another tea bag. The water is already hot." Ida was as good as her word. She arrived at the table with a tea bag and the tea kettle to replenish my cup.

We all gathered around the table for lunch. Meals were becoming the hub of the day. I was beginning to feel closed in. I was used to walking on the treadmill twice a day. My workouts were suffering. Everyone was feeling the strain. I hoped the captain could come up with something soon.

After lunch, the guys did the dishes leaving the three of us women to our own devices. I took up my crochet hook. The afghan I was making would be finished tonight. Sally Mae started a new book. Ida found her knitting. Sally Mae discovered a music station on the TV and put on some easy listening music. It played softly in the background. When the guys finished they headed to the office. Tom telling JJ, he was having trouble not thinking of him as Bubba anymore, he'd show him some basic computer skills.

It looked to me like this was going to become our routine. Breakfast, work on something, lunch, idle work, then puzzle, or board game. I was going to go nuts. I like solitude, but also I like to have the option to walk outside. I'm not someone who wants to be inside all day, every day.

My mind wandered to the case we were working. We'd proven Bobby James' murderer was a police officer who made it look like it was a militia hit or murder by his best friend. Well, we saved a life there. Sally Mae was with us so she was safe and cleared in Bobby James' murder. She would now live with the loss for the rest of her life. Ida Appleton had the closure she needed however she will always wonder if her son would have lived had he received medical attention. How do we put Riley here on the farm with Mike and why did he have to die? What did Riley think Mike knew or would say? Did Riley believe his long time partner had betrayed him to us? Is it why he put an end to Jeff's life? We were missing something and it was going to be the key to getting us sprung.

I took my afghan and crochet hook to the bedroom then knocked on the door of the office.

"Enter."

I went in. Tom and JJ were setting up e-mail for JJ. They both looked up. JJ stood sensing I had something to discuss with Tom.

"I'll go see what's on TV. I can tell you need to talk police business," JJ said excusing himself.

"Thanks, JJ." I said.

"What's up, Macy?" Tom wanted to know.

"Aside from having cabin fever, I think we're missing something here. Why did Riley need to kill Mike? He had never said anything to anyone about what went on the night Bobby James was killed. What was his motivation? What was he going to gain? How did he get on and off the property without being seen?"

"Those are some of the questions I posed to the captain. I don't have it worked out yet either. I guess you have something else?" he raised an eyebrow in question.

"Why did Jeff have to die? They'd been partners for years. Whatever Riley held over his head had kept him quiet. Even Bubba, I mean JJ, sensed there was something amiss between them. What did Jeff do with the money he got? He sure didn't spend it. He didn't send it to Angela. What is pushing Riley to kill now? He'd gotten away with the Bobby James' murder. Did he think we'd have found him if he hadn't killed Mike and Jeff?" The questions were making me as crazy as the confinement.

"I honestly don't know. He's never been my favorite person. He's always seemed a little too brutal and a lot shady."

"What are we going to do? I've gotten into every website which would have information on him. I don't know how to get into his head," I confessed.

"Macy, you're going to make yourself crazy. The captain is just starting his meeting. We have to give him some time to pick the brains of our colleagues and the State Police. I know waiting stinks. There's nothing else we can do for the moment. Let's go start a puzzle. It'll take your mind off this," Tom suggested.

I laughed and we headed toward the living room. When we got there, we found JJ and Sally Mae had the same idea. They were busy working on a puzzle on the card table Sally Mae had found. Ida was watching a soap opera and knitting. Tom and I joined them at the puzzle table.

CHAPTER TWENTY-FOUR

The afternoon was spent between the puzzle, board games, and other individual pursuits. It was pleasant and the underlying tension in the room seemed to somewhat dissipate. There was no bickering and no one seemed to be out of sorts.

Compared to my previous state I was less antsy. I was hoping to hear from the captain by dinner time, but Tom's phone didn't ring. I excused myself and went to the office and opened my laptop to search for an e-mail from the captain. We were missing something and it would nag at me until we found it. Unfortunately I found nothing. I shut it down and went to the bedroom. I had to do something.

Since I was bored out of my mind, I thought it would be a good idea to revisit a few of the details from the case. I grabbed a yellow legal pad and pen then plopped on the bed. Determined to find the missing piece of information, I quietly reviewed the details in my head. As interesting facts came to mind, I made a point to jot them down. Then, I remembered Jeff's notebook. Previously I'd only read what he'd written about the Appleton case. Just then, it dawned on me the key would be in the unread information. Excited about the potential new discovery, I got comfortable and started reading the older cases. I needed to know what Jeff knew.

It was getting dark in my room when Ida came in. She carried a sandwich and a cup of tea. She also turned on a light. I looked up realizing my stomach was rumbling and it was later than I thought.

"I thought you were busy so I didn't have them get you for dinner. I brought you a little something," Ida explained.

"I'm sorry, I didn't realize it was so late." I took the plate and noticed there was also a cup of soup and crackers, and a couple of cookies, chocolate chip were my favorite. I felt bad she had gone to extra trouble for me. "Next time call me, it's not necessary to wait on me."

Ida turned. "It's no trouble, I'll be back in a while to get your dishes. You just keep working. I know it's important."

"Thank you, Ida." She had taken to mothering us all in her own way.

I snacked on my food as I read. It was about half an hour later when I let out a whoop to signify I found what I was looking for. At least, I thought I found it. I gathered up all my notes, the notebook, my dishes, and headed for the kitchen.

I put my dishes in the sink and said, "Gather round I think I know what was going on with Riley."

Everyone grabbed a cup of coffee and gathered around the table. I proceeded to tell them, when I read Jeff's notebook, I only read what concerned the Appleton case. Tonight I decided to read the rest. Tom looked abashed. It made me think he only read the part about the Appleton case, too.

"Hear me out, I have a theory. There was a hit and run accident about four years before Bobby James went missing. It seems to me Riley somehow set up Jeff and then took the rap for it. Claiming he was drinking and didn't realize he hit anyone. He took a suspension and was demoted to patrolman. In reality, it was Jeff driving the car and he wanted to stop. Both of them had been drinking. After, when Riley stole something from evidence and sold it he took the largest cut and made sure Dunning also got a cut. Dunning put the money in a box and left it. Then, he decided there was too much money in the box and he had to do something with it. It's why he set up a trust fund for JJ here." I looked directly at JJ and said, "The money will all be yours."

When his wife, Molly was killed, Dunning was distraught. He threatened to take the money in to the captain and confess the whole thing. He suspected, but could not prove, Riley had been driving the car that killed Molly. There was a change in their partnership and camaraderie. My theory is when Mike turned up dead and we were looking into the Appleton case again, Dunning wanted to come clean. It's why he gave us the notebook. He must have known Riley had killed Bobby James and tried to pin it on Bubba, sorry I mean JJ, I'm still getting used to the name change."

Anyway by giving us the notebook, it left us free to find the truth about Bobby James and point us toward the killer of Mike. I don't think he expected to be killed himself," I finished letting the others digest what I told them.

Tom was quick to jump in, "I wish I'd thought to read the rest. We have the reason Jeff was killed and it's written in his own hand. What we don't have is why he killed Mike, or how he got onto the farm without being seen."

JJ who spoke up, "Look at us hidden out here on the farm. I was able to get onto the farm at night. It's just as easy to get on the farm during the day." JJ smirked in a smug manner as he turned to Ida and asked, "Mrs. A, what happened the morning Mike was killed?"

"Let me think," she pondered a moment then said, "Macy came out to interview me about Bobby James. We talked for a long time."

"So, you were sitting in the house. Did you notice anyone drive in or out?" JJ's excitement heightened as the clues of the case began to unravel.

"No, it wasn't important at the time. I was sure Mike had left and when we walked out his truck wasn't here."

"At any time while you and Macy were talking, someone could have driven onto the farm and concealed a car or truck. They could also have driven off before you noticed Mike's truck back here, too."

"That's probably true," Ida nodded her head in agreement with JJ.

"Here's what I think. Mike was killed before Macy left. I bet the killer drove his truck off the farm and returned it later. At the time, the killer went through Mike's house and truck to see if he had any information which could incriminate him. Then he wiped the truck clean and returned to the farm. Then the killer walked off this property to his own car or truck hidden in a turn off along the road."

"Macy, who was the first officer on the scene?" Tom asked anxiously.

"Oh, my, gosh! It was Riley. He had to have been close. He couldn't have been happy Mrs. Appleton had requested me."

"It's why you are in more danger than anyone in this room," Tom said quietly.

"Great. How do we get him to come after me without endangering everyone here?" It was the biggest challenge.

"I don't know, but I'm going to send your findings to the captain and follow it up with a call."

"Here I thought I was finding a way to get us out of here," I muttered.

"Everything you have done has gotten us closer to being safe again. You've found a new home for JJ's mother and Sally Mae. In addition, you've found additional money for JJ, his mother, and Sally Mae. You've discovered who killed my son, Mike, and Jeff. On top of all that, you've given me the opportunity to help JJ start his new life, by allowing me to give him a job and place to live. I might even feel safer with him here on the farm," Ida said trying to make me see I had done a good thing.

"She's right, you know none of this would have happened if you and Tom hadn't been put on this case. Officer Riley might have bought someone else off. I could be dead by now and JJ could be looking at a life in prison. You have done enough. Let the others take over," Sally Mae added her own brand of logic.

I nodded they were both right. Not used to living with so many people or being inside all day every day, I was finding myself confined. Normally, I engaged in quite a bit of exercise and loved walking. I missed my weights this was starting to get on my nerves.

"Sally Mae, what was the substance taped inside your toilet?" I asked curiously.

She laughed. "I wondered if you were ever going to ask about it. Mike took flour and sugar and poured them in a baggie and taped it to the inside of the lid. He said it would make you think drugs had been involved. He thought it would buy us time to get away."

"I'm sure the boys in the lab had fun with it. We didn't much give it any thought," was my response.

Tom came back into the room. "There was some table salt and baking soda in it too. Mike had a real keen sense of humor. The captain says they are going back over every case Riley worked on. They are tearing apart the evidence logs and the evidence room to see what has been stolen over the years. IA is combing every one of his bank accounts. They had the accounts frozen so he can't get to the money. They're also crawling all over his house. He can't go back there either.

He's going to get desperate and start looking for a place to stay. Macy, you aren't going to like this, but we need to go back to three hour night shifts." Tom was frowning as he said it.

"I'd like to take one of those shifts. I'm very capable of handling myself with an intruder," JJ offered eager to get in some action.

"It's a nice thought, JJ, but he's going to be armed," Tom looked at him as he said it.

"I know I'm not supposed to have weapons, but I've never killed anything but a deer with a gun. The man who died in Kentucky had come at me with a broken beer bottle. I was defending myself. In fact, I don't remember how I got the bottle away from him. I just remember hitting him. I could hold my own against Drew. I know where his soft spots are. I don't need a gun."

"I think you should all calm down. I'm not able to fend off anyone, so if you three plan to guard us tonight, I'll put on a fresh pot of coffee and I'll make sure the tea kettle is full. Then I'm taking this old woman to bed. God be with you." Ida did just what she said she was going to do.

When we heard her door close, Sally Mae said, "I'm a light sleeper. You can wake me and I can get Mrs. Appleton into the safe room if there is any trouble."

"Sally Mae can also handle a gun, so I'll make sure she has my secondary weapon. Let me take the first shift. I'm fired up because of what I found. I can spend the time pacing."

Tom laughed. "Okay, Macy has the first three hours. JJ, do you want to take the second shift?"

"Yeah, I do," his eagerness showing as he grinned from ear to ear.

"Then you need to save me some coffee and I'll take the third shift. Since I don't like the idea of anyone facing Riley unarmed, I'm going to give you my secondary weapon. It's not a parole violation if you're in police custody which technically you are."

"Whatever. I'm sure I could take him," JJ assured Tom. He beamed with the trust Tom was putting in him.

"If it's all the same to you I'm going to make the most of my sleep time. I'll see you all in the morning."

They headed to bed and I made myself a path so I could pace. I also checked the doors, knowing no one had come in or out of them since last night. It was going to be a long night and I was the prime target this time. I wondered where Riley might go to hide out. There were plenty of places, vacant barns and businesses where no one would think to look. Would he come here to the scene of two of his crimes? Would he try to find Mrs. Appleton? Was he even looking for Sally Mae? I was going to keep playing all these questions repeatedly in my head. Something was still missing, something besides Riley.

CHAPTER TWENTY-FIVE

I was sitting at the table engaged in a puzzle when JJ came to relieve me. I made sure the coffee was hot. He looked ready to start his shift.

"I appreciate you and Tom trusting me with a gun. I really don't think it's necessary though," he told me.

"I believe it *is* necessary. Riley is not someone to mess with. If he comes here, he'll try the doors or he'll break a window. I'm just hoping he stays away."

As I headed to my room, I noticed Sally Mae was sleeping and there was no sound from Ida's room. Once I slipped into my sweats and slid under the sheets it didn't take me long to fall asleep.

I awoke to find Sally Mae standing over me. She put her finger to her lips as a cue to remain quiet. Suddenly I was instantly alert.

"What is it?" I asked in a whisper.

"I'm not sure. JJ came back and woke me. I'm going to get Ida. Will you open the safe room?"

Without saying a word, I dropped to the floor, rolled back the rug, and opened the lock. By the time Sally Mae came back with Ida, I was turning the light on down in the safe room. Once Sally Mae helped her down the stairs I closed and locked the door.

I was in stealth mode as I slipped down the hallway staying in the shadows. To my surprise, I saw someone in the other hall. I was relieved to find it was Tom. Wordlessly, I fell into a crouch where I could see the living room. JJ was there with a small light on. Once he saw me he waved. Tom and I both entered the room and stood in awe. Lying with his hands cuffed behind his back on the kitchen floor was Riley. I was stunned. Here trussed up like a pig was the man police were trying to find.

"How did you manage this?" I questioned JJ with intensity.

"I heard something out by the garbage cans. I remembered you seeing a bear out there one night so, I hit all the lights and looked out window. I was shocked to see Riley out there. He stumbled against the garbage can and was trying to pick it up. I didn't waste any time nailing him. Within seconds I was out the door then, I cracked him on the head. As he was going down I caught him and cuffed him with his own cuffs."

"His own cuffs? Now, that's a good move." I was impressed with JJ's skills.

"Yeah, I learned from the best," he snickered then continued his story. "I didn't want to alarm Mrs. A so I had Sally Mae take her to the safe room. Then, I went to wake Tom. What do we do next?"

I glanced at the clock and noticed it was 3 a.m. Tom was already dialing the phone. I wondered if he dialed 9-1-1 or the captain. I got my answer when he spoke.

"Captain, this is Maxwell. We've apprehended Riley at the Appleton farm. He's unconscious and handcuffed. You can send as many as you want, it's not necessary to run sirens. See you soon," his voice was very professional for someone who had been asleep only moments before.

He hung up his phone and turned to us, "Bring Ida and Sally Mae up from the safe room. They will want to dress before the department arrives. I'm going to finish dressing. JJ, can you watch over him without inflicting any more pain?" He smiled at JJ as if to say, you've got this under control.

"Sure can, Tom. I'll even start a fresh pot of coffee," JJ joked.

Tom headed for his room and I went to mine. I unlocked the safe room and helped both women come up, then told them they had about five minutes to get dressed because soon the farm would be flooded with local and state police. I also shared the media would most likely show up as well. Each of us took the time to quickly make ourselves presentable and then headed back to the kitchen.

Ida took a quick look Riley who was still lying on the floor but slowly coming around. Then she headed for the kitchen to prepare to feed an army. Tom, JJ, and Sally Mae finished the pot of coffee so Ida put on a fresh pot. I put the kettle on and found myself a tea bag. We needed to be fortified for the onslaught.

Ida poured cups of coffee and I took my tea to the table. As I walked toward it a fully awakened Riley used his legs to try and trip me. It was his first mistake. To retaliate I threw the hot tea in his face and tried to brace myself for the fall. Thankfully, JJ grabbed me by the arm and I caught my balance. Riley howled like a banshee from the pain of his face. Instinctively, Ida reached for a towel and some ice cubes. Just then, someone knocked on the door.

From the other side of the closed door the captain yelled out, "Captain Wellington. Rivers Edge Police. Open the door!"

Tom sprinted to the door. As he opened it, Ida tried to apply ice to Riley's face. He let out another ear-piercing howl.

"What the hell?" the Captain said.

"Come on in, Captain. You came at a great time," Tom said sarcastically. "Riley tried to trip Macy and she was carrying a cup of hot tea. As you can see his face has been burned."

"It serves him right. He should have known she had something hot. When I heard him cry out, I ordered an ambulance. I wasn't taking any chances. The State Police should be here any minute." The captain paused to look around, "Nice place here."

Sally Mae offered the captain a cup of coffee. JJ managed to get Riley to a chair. He had taken rope and tied his legs to it, so he was pretty much hog tied. The captain came to the table.

Tom introduced him to Ida Appleton, Sally Mae Davis and Jeffrey Joseph (JJ) Waxman.

The yard filled with police cars all with lights flashing. Tom and the captain took their coffees and went out to greet those coming. Sally Mae took a tray out with cups of steaming coffee. Ida began cooking breakfast for an army, she started with bacon. While it was cooking she shredded the potatoes for hash browns. JJ and I kept an eye on our prisoner.

By the time Sally Mae returned with the empty cups, Ida had pancakes going and eggs ready to scramble. Sally Mae began making toast. Ida had biscuits in the oven and sausage ready to slice for gravy. I was astounded at how quick she put everything together. Jointly, they set plates on the table and food on the counter. Ida went to the door and banged two pans together once. The yard went quiet.

"Form a line, I have breakfast for everyone." She turned and came back to the kitchen. She had more pancakes on and extra eggs cooking.

We let the men and women file through the kitchen. Sally Mae had washed up the cups and they were filled with fresh coffee. Each took a plate, silverware, and a cup of coffee. They sat at the table or took the food outside. It was orderly and over in about five minutes. Those who finished came back in and set their utensils in the sink. Sally Mae washed them continuously. When the rush seemed over, Ida brought food to the table. Sally Mae brought plates and silverware.

"Gentlemen, the ladies and I are ready to eat," she announced.

Tom, Captain Wellington and a man from the State Police I didn't recognize came to the table. JJ and I joined them. Sally Mae and Ida served breakfast and then joined us. Introductions were made all around including Ed Winston from the State Police. As we began eating we heard the first sounds from our prisoner.

"Are you just going to eat in front of me? I got rights. You can't do that."

Ed Winston spoke up, "You'll get your bread and water when we're done. Hold your tongue or I'll order you gagged."

The meal was pleasant. There was no talk of the interrogation yet to come. By the time we finished eating, most of the officers who had been outside were gone. The only ones left were the few who would escort the transport vehicle when Riley was loaded into it.

Ida and Sally Mae were again on clean up duty when a paramedic was brought in to look at Riley's face. He applied some cream and said it should be applied twice a day. Then he left.

Ida asked if she could return to her home. Ed Winston told her he believed she would be safe there. She took Sally Mae and the two of them left for her house. I could only imagine what they might have to talk about.

Riley was pulled up to the table. Each of the men had fresh coffee; I had a cup of tea. It was time to start grilling Riley on his behavior.

"I want a lawyer. I have been subjected to police brutality. I was struck from behind and bound. Then I had hot stuff thrown on my face. I have the burns to prove it. I'm going to sue all of you," the redness on his face from the burn gave credit to his outburst.

"Sue away, Riley. We're going to ask you some questions," Ed Winston said curtly.

"I'm not answering a thing without my lawyer," Riley said firmly.

JJ was not having this. "Answer me one thing, Drew. Why did you kill Bobby James? I sent you to help him."

Riley looked at JJ for the first time. "You, worthless kid trying to leach off Dunning. Don't know how you convinced him he was your pappy. He woulda never had a worthless kid like you. Do you know who your mama is?" Riley sneered.

It took all JJ's control not to leap from his chair and deck the man. "I didn't have to convince Jeff he was my dad, he'd known it since I was born. He paid my mom support while I was growing up. What I don't understand is why you wanted me to look like a killer?"

"I heard tell it's what you are. Man who beats people to death if they cross him. Even heard you done time for killing someone," Riley smirked in spite of his burned face.

"You heard right. I did time. I've paid my debt and I've changed. I'm going to make something of myself," JJ said defiantly.

"Not likely. Ain't no one in these parts will trust you enough to hire you. You'll be back to petty theft and killing before you know it," Riley was gaining confidence.

"You'd lose that bet," Tom said calmly. "Macy and I will speak to JJ's good name. He's already got a job and a place to live. He's going to be more productive than you could ever be."

"What fool would hire a convict?" Riley's laugh was raucous.

"Mrs. Appleton has hired him as a full-time farm hand. She also offered him this bunkhouse to live in. He'll start as soon as he gets the stench of you out of here," I assured him. My dislike of the man was growing by the moment.

"That old woman would hire the kid who beat her son almost to death. She's nuttier than I thought. Don't worry, you'll screw up and I'll be there to arrest you," Riley sneered.

Ed Winston spoke then point. "Your days of arresting people are over, Riley. You are under investigation in two murders, one attempted murder, for your looting of the Rivers Edge property room, and for trespassing here. You will probably die in jail."

"I'm not going to jail. You can't prove a thing," his confidence made him puff out his chest.

"Actually, he's looking at three murders, since there is no statute of limitations on murder. He's going to be tried for the death of Bobby James Appleton. I believe he's also going to be charged with hindering an investigation." Captain Wellington sneered at Riley.

"Where's my lawyer? I haven't got nothin' to say," Riley said again.

"Macy, would you like to do the honors?" the Captain asked.

I pulled my Miranda card from my pocket and began reading Riley his rights. "Drew Riley, you are under arrest for the murders of Bobby James Appleton, Mike West, Jeff Dunning, the attempted murder of Captain Wellington, hindering a police investigation, robbing the property room, and trespassing."

He sneered at me saying, "Listen chick, you aren't speaking clearly."

I raised my voice a bit and continued, "You have the right to remain silent. Anything you say can and will be used against you in a court of law. You have the right to an attorney, if you cannot afford one, one will be appointed.

"I already asked for my lawyer. I don't have to say another thing," he spat.

When I was done, I asked, "Do you understand your rights?"

"Yeah, bitch, I do. Too, bad you had someone like Bubba here to rescue you when I tripped you," he was becoming openly belligerent.

I ignored his comment. The men picked up Riley chair and all and took him to the yard. There he was removed from the chair and placed in the back of a squad car. I, for one, was glad to see him go. I went back into the bunkhouse to finish the clean up. It was time to pack my bags and return to my home.

JJ and Tom followed behind me. They carried the chair vacated by Riley. We put the puzzle back in the box and started straightening up. I told the guys to bring me all the bedding and I would begin the laundry.

Sally Mae and Ida showed up after the last police car had pulled out. Sally Mae took over with the laundry. While Ida found food for sandwiches. We would have our last meal in the bunkhouse as a make shift family. I took my bag to my car and pulled it out so I could get in and drive away. The afghan I made, I gave to Ida. She thanked me with tears in her eyes.

JJ was going to have enough food for months. Between what we had purchased and what was in the safe room, food would not be a problem. He thought he would use the room he had shared with Tom. It just seemed right to him.

We ate together talking about what we would all do now. I would get ready to attend my niece Kaitlyn's graduation. I would be among family. Of course, I'd go back to work and when the time came. I'd testify at Riley's trial. Life would become normal.

Tom was going home to spend some time with his wife and boys. He would be there for the birth of his third child. He would be at work on the same reports I'd be working on and waiting for his turn to testify. Life for him would be normal, too.

Sally Mae was going to use the college classes she had taken to find a new job. She would move into Mike's house and take care of his mother. It was going to be enough change for her for now. She also knew she would be welcome to spend time with Ida.

JJ was going to start working on the farm tomorrow. He was going to do his best to make his friend Bobby James proud. He might even take some courses at the community college. He heard they had courses in small engine repair. He would help his mom move to Rivers Edge and take up life in Jeff's house. She wasn't going to have to work again and he would make her proud. He was leaving bad boy "Bubba" behind.

Ida was going back to life as normal with many more friends. She thought it was time she renewed her friendship with Mike's mom. Sally Mae was welcome to come anytime. Between them they would make sure JJ had regular meals. She also wanted to meet his mom. Tom and I were invited to stop by anytime. I knew I would call ahead but, I would stop by. Tom and I walked to our cars. I followed him to Hank's Car Rental where he turned in the car we rented and received a voucher to turn in for payment.

I dropped him at home. He called ahead and the boys were waiting on the porch for us to arrive.

"You want to come in, Macy?" he asked.

"Not this time. I'll check on Shannon later this week," I promised.

Tom nodded as he gathered the boys in his arms. When he let them go they raced each other to the front door. I backed out the driveway and headed for home.

My neighbors had picked up my papers and mail. It was sitting on the steps heading into the house from the garage. The yard had been mowed. Yes, I was home. First, thing I did was take a long hot bath. I soaked until the water grew cold. Soaping myself up, I decided to drained the tub and shower the suds off. After drying off, I pulled on a pair of sweats, made a cup of tea and curled up to go through the mail. It was nice to be home.

CHAPTER TWENTY-SIX

I dozed off for a while and was startled out of my sleep. I wasn't sure what had woken me. To my surprise I was alarmed to hear someone moving in my kitchen going through the drawers. I pulled my gun from the sofa cushion and headed for the noise. Slowly I eased myself toward the kitchen with my gun raised. If necessary, I'd shoot first and ask questions later. To my surprise, Tom, Shannon, Sally Mae, Ida, and JJ stood in the middle of my kitchen.

"What on earth? I could have shot you all," I yelled in a chastising tone embarrassed at being caught sleeping in my sweats.

"We knew you wouldn't think about eating tonight. So, we got together and made you dinner. Shannon learned how to decorate a cake from Sally Mae," Tom said sheepishly.

Together they all shouted, "Happy Birthday, Macy."

I had lost track of time and forgotten it was *my* birthday. I lowered the gun and began to cry. It had been a long time since I celebrated my birthday with anyone. Here they stood with dinner and gifts. It didn't take long for them to circle me, giving out hugs letting me feel the love and camaraderie which had been built in the past week.

I told Sally Mae where to find dishes and silverware. The table was set, wine was poured, and we enjoyed a feast. Ida had outdone herself again mashed potatoes, gravy, tender pork roast, green beans, and spinach salad. It was delightful to have dinner with friends. I even got over my embarrassment at being caught sleeping in my sweats. The wine and laughter flowed. Shannon explained she baked the cake and supervised as Sally Mae worked her magic to make it stunning.

We moved to my living room with coffee and wine to open presents. Sally Mae had gotten me several bottles of nail polish. She included a note promising to teach me how to paint my nails. Ida put in a lace table cloth she made with her own hands. JJ had gone with Sally Mae and picked out a bottle of my favorite perfume. Tom and Shannon had purchased a sweat suit for me. Tom chuckled saying it was time for a new one. Shannon took my hand and whispered, "Forgive me." I nodded because there was nothing to forgive.

While I was opening packages, Ida disappeared to the kitchen. The next thing I knew they were all singing 'Happy Birthday.' JJ took the candle lit cake from Ida and put it in front of me.

"Make a wish, birthday girl. We are waiting for a piece of this cake."

I laughed, blew out the candles, and made a wish. Although I'd never admit to it, I wished we would always be friends. Life was not lonely with friends.

Ida served the cake with ice cream in the dining room. When we finished eating, Sally Mae, Shannon, and Ida cleaned up. While they worked, Tom and JJ took me to the living room. I sensed they needed to tell me something.

"Macy, I hate to bring work into a celebration, but you need to stay with one of us," Tom started.

"Why would I need to stay with anyone? I've not even been home for a day. No one could possibly be out to get me," I was confused.

"Someone could. Riley escaped before they got him to the jail. He messed up the officers pretty bad and has both of their weapons. We think he might come after you."

"Great, just what I wanted to hear. Where am I going to stay I won't be putting someone risk? Ida surely can't protect me, nor could Sally Mae although she'd be good back up. I can't stay with you and Shannon. I don't want to put Shannon and the boys in danger. I'm open for suggestions." I groaned.

"Stay at the bunkhouse with me, Macy. Don't argue, the captain has even asked that a State Police officer be assigned to stay there," JJ said.

I looked at both of them. This could not be happening. What JJ said, made sense. I just didn't want to be a burden to anyone. I took a deep breath and nodded.

"Okay, JJ, you have a house guest. Who is going to keep Ida and Sally Mae safe?" I agreed.

"Did I forget to mention they are staying in the bunkhouse, too?"

"Before you ask, I'm not. A State Police officer will be staying with Shannon, the boys, and me. We also get the benefit of one assigned outside," Tom said quickly.

"Let me change and pack a bag any idea how many days this time?" I said resigned to going back.

"Indefinitely, but remember there's a washing machine and dryer," JJ added.

I laughed and headed upstairs. Everyone was ready to go when I came down. I rode with JJ, Sally Mae, and Ida. Tom and Shannon headed home to their boys. The boys were going to love being part of a spy game.

I wasn't surprised to see the beds had been made up and made my way to the back bedroom. This time I would have it to myself. Sally Mae was staying in the room we'd used as an office and Ida had her own room. We had an officer in the living room and JJ was at the other end. Yes, this was almost as good as home.

The detective in me wanted to know how on earth Riley had out maneuvered two officers and gotten away when there was an escort. Someone was going to be in hot water for this. I was wound up and unable to sleep so I paced the bedroom, knowing everyone else had called it a day. I decided maybe a cup of tea would help so, I threw on my robe and headed to the kitchen.

"I'm sorry I didn't mean to disturb you. I couldn't sleep and thought a cup of tea might calm me," I explained to the dark haired officer sitting on the sofa with a book.

"Go ahead. I'm just reading. I think I've had enough coffee to keep me awake for a week. At least it's better than the swill at the office." He chuckled.

His comment about the coffee brought a chuckle from me. Tom complained about office coffee all the time. I was glad I didn't drink the stuff. I went about making my tea.

"I'm sorry, I'm, Eli Patterson," he said rising to join me in the kitchen.

"Macy McVannel," I replied. His deep blue eyes were compelling. "Nice to meet you, whose bad side are you on that you got this duty?"

"Actually, I volunteered," he said honestly.

I was surprised. Most officers tried to hide when protection duty was being assigned. "I'm impressed. Most officers run when this kind of job comes up.

"You didn't. You protected three people to bag a bad guy," he said letting me know he knew what had happened.

"I didn't know when I started my assignment I was going to be protecting three people. Luck is what brought Sally Mae and JJ here. It wasn't even good police work," I admitted. "Ida got dragged into it because she was kind enough to let Tom and I stay here."

"It doesn't matter how they ended up here, you and Tom were willing to put your lives on the line to protect them," his sincerity had me blushing.

I had done my job and wasn't looking for praise. I finished making my tea and asked, "So what are you reading?" I asked hoping to change the subject.

"A *James Patterson* novel," he chuckled. "One would think I'd get enough of police work so I wouldn't have to read about it."

"I love his work. He makes what we do seem so simple, yet compelling," was my enthusiastic reply.

"He's gripping, I'll give him that," Eli conceded.

Eli was interesting, well read, and amusing. We talked novels and writers for the next couple hours. It just seemed natural. When the coffee pot was empty, I washed it out and started another pot. I washed my tea cup.

"Thanks for talking to me. I think I'll be able to sleep now," I said as I headed toward my room.

"Glad to be of service. Happy Birthday, Macy," he said smiling.

Again I blushed and asked, "How did you know?"

"Ida offered me a piece of birthday cake earlier and mentioned it," he said.

I made my way down the hall to my room thinking of his smile. Amazingly, I was asleep before my head hit the pillow. I slept like someone with no worries in the world.

Sally Mae came into my room around 8:30 a.m., "Hey sleepy head, are you getting up anytime soon? Ida's got breakfast ready to go on the table."

I rolled over and stretched. "I'll be there in just a minute." I quickly grabbed clothing and headed to take a shower. Ten minutes, later I presented myself in the kitchen. I took a seat at the table which happened to be next to Eli. Ida served up one of her famous breakfasts and I could see my workout regime going out the window. Again, I was going to be confined to the bunkhouse 24/7. I shrugged and dug into the food. Conversation floated around me. I was comfortable but still a bit tired.

"Macy, you are quiet this morning," Ida said her motherly instincts kicking in.

"I'm sorry, Ida, I was up late last night," I replied.

"It's my fault. Macy just wanted a cup of tea and I pulled her into conversation. I should have let her sleep, but I enjoyed her company," Eli smiled as he explained.

I found myself blushing again. This was becoming a bad habit. I continued to eat.

Sally Mae and Ida cleared the table as I finished a second cup of tea. Eli had gone to shower and get some shut eye because he had the third shift again tonight. JJ had pulled out the card table and reassembled the puzzle we had been working on so I wandered over to work on it for a while.

Sally Mae came over, "Want to talk, Macy?"

"Not really. It was nice of you all to remember my birthday. I enjoyed dinner last night but, I didn't pack any of the nail polish," I said distractedly.

Sally Mae laughed, "I knew you'd forget so I grabbed them. Shall we practice now?"

"It might be fun," I said warming to the idea.

Sally Mae went to her room and came back with the package of polish. "So do you want to go brash or shall we start timid?"

"Is there something in between?" I queried.

"I thought you'd never ask." She opened the package and said, "At the kitchen table we don't want to spill any on the puzzle.

I quickly moved. I'm right-handed so Sally Mae did my right hand. Then she handed me the bottle and led me through doing the left. It wasn't bad for someone who had never done it before. Sally Mae produced a nail dryer and I had finished nails in an instant. I had found it relaxing which surprised me.

I took the bottles back to my room and found the yarn I grabbed. It was time to start the layette for Shannon. Since they didn't know the sex of the baby I'd chosen a variegated baby yarn. I went back to the living room and sat on the sofa. Ida was on the sofa with me doing her knitting and watching her soap opera. Sally Mae and JJ were working on the puzzle. I settled in. It was going to be a long day.

Two hours later, Eli joined us. By then I had finished a hat and sweater and started the afghan. I picked up my things and took them to the bedroom. When I came back out I joined Sally

Mae in the kitchen and we got lunch underway. Ida let us take over today. She continued knitting, although she changed the channel to headline news.

The local news came on as Sally Mae and I set food on the table. Drew Riley was the headline. His photo was shone, along with the warning he was armed and dangerous. They flashed an eight hundred number along the bottom of the screen. It was a comfort to know we had driven him to ground. Since he was well known in the community, he would have trouble finding someplace to lay low. I wondered if he would come back to the bunkhouse, knowing JJ was be living here. It made me think because he would be looking for me and I hoped my neighbors didn't get any fallout from this.

We muted the TV and settled in at the table to a lively conversation. JJ noting he was already a day behind in his work. Ida laughed and told him it would be there when he was able to do it. Eli told us he followed his father into the police force. It was then I remembered hearing about a Patterson who was killed in the line. I didn't mention it now, but would ask him about it later. Sally Mae also managed to get out of him, he was single. I forced myself to keep my head down and focused on my food.

I started to clean up lunch and Eli joined me. He grabbed a towel and started drying dishes. I told him where things went and he put them away. Ida had gone back to her room. JJ and Sally Mae were at the puzzle. The only thing missing was Tom, although I had to admit Eli was a nice addition.

I went to find my phone needing a reality check. First, I called Tom to see how things were going. He assured me all was well there. My next call was to the captain. They were following Riley. He broke into Mike's house, but had not damaged anything. Seems he was looking for food and didn't find any. He was by his house, but it was cordoned off by police tape and a state car was parked out front. The officer radioed in a suspicious car with a description and license plate. It was found near Jeff's later, but it had not been broken into because it was also cordoned off by police tape with an officer on duty there. They also took the precaution of posting an officer at Mrs. West's house though she was still staying with her sister. They were even patrolling by JJ's mother's house. She had not been brought into the loop yet and they felt she was essentially safe. There was nothing to do but hunker down. All of the information Tom and I found had been turned over to the District Attorney and they were busy building a case so they could prosecute. Riley's breaking out was going to be added to the charges. I thanked the captain for the information and ended the call.

I headed back to the living room. Ida had been quiet at lunch and had not come back out. She was usually the energizer bunny. I hoped she was feeling all right. I worried all this might be too much for her. I planned to check on her if she didn't appear soon.

"Hey, Macy, did you talk to Tom?" JJ wanted to know.

"Yes, and the captain, too there's not too much to tell. Tom, Shannon, and the boys have inside and outside officers. JJ, they're patrolling near your mom's to be on the safe side. Jeff's place is covered, too. They spotted Riley near his house, but didn't try to apprehend him. He ditched the car he was driving. There is someone patrolling at Mike's mom's house. Sorry, to tell you they got to Mike's too late but is someone there now. Riley had gotten in, but didn't do any damage. He was looking for food. The DA's office is building a case they can take to trial and we will all be asked to testify. Pretty much we're here for a while."

"Here isn't all bad, Macy," Eli commented. "You know you're safe."

Ida had come into the room while I was talking. She looked a bit drawn. I was still worried about her. "Ida, do you want coffee or some of the lemonade you made earlier?"

"Lemonade, please, Macy."

I got her a glass of lemonade and took it to where she sat. As I handed her the glass I asked, "Ida, are you feeling alright?"

"I'm a little tired. There's been a lot of excitement. I'll be fine. I need to rest more," she replied.

"Okay, but you let me know if you need anything. We can get you a doctor," I assured her.

"I'm sure it's just the excitement."

Sally Mae had heard our exchange. She came to me in the kitchen. "Do you think we should be worried about Ida?"

"Not yet, but you and I should plan to do the cooking and clean up for a couple of days." Sally Mae nodded and went back to her puzzle. Eli nodded letting me know he, too had heard my conversation with Ida. With us looking out for her, I felt she would get through this. I turned in the kitchen and started pulling things from the cupboards and fridge to start working on dinner. It served to keep me occupied. Eli moved to the table to talk to Ida.

Dinner wasn't as exciting as some of our other meals but we kept the conversation moving. Ida again seemed quiet and I noticed she didn't eat much. After dinner Sally Mae and JJ started cleaning up. Eli found himself with nothing to do and wandered to the puzzle. Ida said she thought she would turn in early. I made a cup of tea and took it to her room. I knocked on the door. She called out for me to come in. She had put on her nightgown and robe and was sitting on the edge of her bed.

"I made you some tea. Are you sure you're okay?" concern filling my voice.

"Thank you, Macy. I will be fine in the morning," she assured me.

"I will check on you later. Just leave the empty cup on the night stand." I closed the door on my way out. Ida had her Bible in front of her and was sipping the tea. I reported back to the others I thought she reached her limit. We needed to really watch her health. I also told them I would check on her later.

As we settled in for the evening the *Scrabble* board came out and we took each other on. After a couple of games, I went to check on Ida. She was sleeping with the Bible on her chest. I moved the Bible to the nightstand, picked up the empty teacup, covered her, and discovered she was burning up. I left the room to alert the others.

"I didn't want to wake her. She's burning up with fever." I was agitated by this turn of events. I had grown very fond of Ida. "This ordeal has taken its toll on her health. We need to give her aspirin, Motrin, or Tylenol every four hours starting the next time she is awake. We are leaving her in bed tomorrow and waiting on her. Lots of liquids and rest I don't want her to end up in the hospital." The whole time I was talking I was pacing.

"Slow down, Macy. We'll take turns keeping an eye on her. No one wants to see her sick," Eli said. He seemed to have grasped the situation well.

"Do you think we should wake her and try to get something down her now?" I asked.

"I don't know, because I don't know what medicine she takes and how it might interact," Eli replied.

"I know," Sally Mae said quietly, "She takes something for high blood pressure."

"Do you know the name of it?" I demanded.

"No, but she goes to Dr. Fritz in town," Sally Mae replied.

"Sally Mae, you are a life saver. I'll call the captain and have him find out what she is taking and what we can give her." I grabbed my cell phone and started punching in the number.

She smiled and started putting the game away. He said he would get right on it. It wasn't ten minutes and I had a call back. We could give her Motrin and cold compresses and keep him apprised of how she was. He had the doctor and an ambulance on standby.

Sally Mae got a bowl and put cool water in it. "I'll give her some Motrin and take the first shift sitting with her and putting compresses on her forehead."

Before anyone could react JJ said, "I have the second shift. Eli, you don't need to take a shift because you are busy keeping us safe. Which leaves you with the last shift, Macy."

"No problem," I replied.

Sally Mae and I headed to Ida's room. She got her to take two Motrin and began to sponge bathe her. I left the room quietly closing the door. I knew things were under control. JJ had headed to bed. He said he would relieve Sally Mae in a couple of hours.

"Guess it leaves the two of us again," Eli said encouragingly.

"Let me get my yarn, we can talk while I work on the layette for Shannon."

"Sounds good." Eli headed to the kitchen. When I returned coffee and tea were sitting on the coffee table in front of the sofa.

"Thank you, that was thoughtful," I smiled being waited on wasn't the norm for me.

"I won't keep you up as late tonight. I know you've got the early hours with Mrs. Appleton," his concern for both Ida and me was touching.

"It's okay. I can function on just a little sleep if need be," I assured him.

We talked about family and how mine had dwindled to just my brother and his family. Eli had a big family and shared them with me. He was interesting and I knew if we had not been thrown together like this we probably never would have met at all. Around midnight I checked on Sally Mae and Ida both were sleeping, Ida fitfully. I left them and went to my room wanting as much sleep as I could get. I felt we were in for more than just Motrin and cold compresses.

I awoke with a start. It was close to 3 am. I got up and quickly dressed in jeans and a t-shirt then went to Ida's room to relieve JJ. He had moved the chair closer to Ida and was holding her hand. He looked up as I entered and shook his head. He tucked her hand back on the bed and motioned me into the hallway.

"I carried Sally Mae to bed when I relieved her. Mrs. A. has been thrashing and calling for Bobby James and his dad. I can't get her fever to break. When she sounded like she was having trouble breathing I found a couple more pillows in the closet and propped her up. Macy, I'm worried. We can't let her die. I have so much to make up to her." He was distraught with worry.

"JJ, she has long forgiven you for any part you had in Bobby James' death. She's delirious so she's calling for people she loved.

I'll keep an eye on her. Do we have thermometer anywhere?" I asked him.

"I don't know, but I'll look. Please Macy, call for an ambulance. We can make it look like Ida's been at home," he pleaded.

"Don't worry, JJ, I have no intentions of letting her die. I've grown to love her very much," I told him.

He nodded and went off to look for a thermometer. I heard him talking to Eli. JJ was scared. If I were honest, so was I. Ida had become important to all of us. She was right, the cloak and dagger stuff was too much for her. I'd wait a couple hours and call the captain. I wanted her some where she could be well cared for.

JJ came back with a thermometer. Carefully we put it in Ida's mouth. I watched the second hand on my watch. After three minutes we took it out. Her temperature was way too high. It registered 103. I left the room and made a call to the captain.

"Wellington," he answered sleepily.

"Captain, this is Macy. We've been giving Mrs. Appleton Motrin every four hours all night. We've also used cold compresses on her forehead. Her temperature is 103. We can't let it get higher or she could have a stroke. We need the ambulance. It's still dark so we are going to carry her to the house, so it will look natural. Eli can stay with her until the ambulance arrives."

"I'll have it rolling in five, Macy. Be careful," he admonished.

I hung up the phone and explained the situation to Eli. He didn't like leaving the three of us alone, but didn't see an option. JJ carried Ida to her house and into her room. He hated leaving her there with Eli, but knew he couldn't risk being seen in the early dawn. I stayed in the shadows to provide cover in case JJ was stopped on the way back to the bunkhouse. JJ made his way quickly back to my side and we were heading for the bunkhouse when I heard a movement in the bushes.

"JJ, stay low and head for the front door," I ordered not waiting to see if he followed my directions. I made for the back of the bunkhouse, it's where Riley had tried to get in the first time. I wanted to head him off. I knew he was armed, but so was I and I had the advantage of knowing the area better than he did. I stayed to the shadows and moved quickly. The noise in the brush had died down. I was wondering if it was our friend the bear. As I reached the backdoor, I heard it open. I took one last look toward the brush and stepped inside.

JJ closed and locked the door. I saw he was armed with the small caliber gun I had given to Sally Mae last week. I had not even thought about the gun after the night we captured Riley. I would be sure to collect it when we were free to go.

"I didn't see anyone or anything," I said breathlessly.

"Probably some coons or a skunk. They're nocturnal animals. It's better to be safe than sorry," he said.

"I agree. Is Sally Mae still sleeping?" I asked.

"Sleep with you all making racket? Not a chance," she chuckled.

I turned to see her coming up from behind the sofa. She was armed with a butcher knife. I laughed. "Sally Mae, you can't put a knife up against a bullet. The bullet wins every time."

JJ cleared his throat to speak, "I don't know about you guys, but I'm hungry. It's been a long night."

Sally Mae looked at him and rolled her eyes. "Men and their stomachs, I can start breakfast, but I'd like to wait until Eli returns. Do you think you can hold it together until then?"

JJ shrugged. "I guess. Besides maybe they can tell him something about what's wrong with Mrs. A."

When it was settled Sally Mae went to the kitchen and started getting things ready to put on when Eli returned. We heard the ambulance arrive then leave about fifteen minutes later. The sun was coming up and Eli should be returning any minute. He promised to lock up the house.

The gunshot broke the morning calm. I was instantly alert. I didn't know if I should go out the front or back door. There was no return fire, was Eli down? I didn't know. My fingers were dialing the captain.

"Gunshots, officer may be down," I shouted into the phone. I turned to Sally Mae and JJ, "Head for the safe room. Shoot first, ask questions later."

They didn't question my order and quickly darted down the hall. I heard a sound at the front door. I hesitated not wanting to make myself a target. It was then I heard my name.

"Macy, it's Eli."

I was at the door and had it opened just as Eli fell in. He had been shot. I kicked the door closed and locked it. I caught him mid-fall.

"Let me get you to the sofa. Did you see who it was?" I was talking rapidly.

"No, shot came out of the bushes. I was too big a target."

"I called the captain when I heard the shot. Told him you might be down. I'm so sorry, Eli. I'd heard something when JJ and I were returning. He must not have been able to pick us out. I should have tried to get back to you." I knew something was off and was blaming myself for this. Then I heard a sound in the hall and looked to see JJ making his way toward me. I wanted to strangle him. He needed to be safe with Sally Mae.

"What do you think you're doing?" I hissed.

"I heard the door open as we were going down. Sally Mae is in the safe room. She's got the rifle down there and she's good with it." He looked at Eli. "Damn, I should have cracked him harder." He turned and went back toward the hall closet. He came back carrying a couple of towels. "Get out of the way, Macy. I don't want him bleeding to death."

I stepped back and watched as he checked out Eli's wound. "It's through and through. It'll be sore, but he won't die."

I felt myself let out a breath I didn't know I'd been holding. I was just getting to know Eli, and I liked what I'd seen. I sure didn't want something to happen to him on my watch. In the distance I could hear the sirens, lots of sirens. This place was going to be flooded with police officers in just a minute.

"I'm going to get Sally Mae." I ran down the hall and opened the door in the floor. "Sally Mae, the cavalry has arrived. Come on out."

She quickly made her way up the stairs. I had put the floor back down and just entered the living room when the captain pounded on the door yelling, "Macy, get this door open!"

I opened the door and the paramedics entered immediately. They started to work on Eli and I gave the captain a brief rundown of what I knew.

"Keep everyone locked in here. I don't want this clown just walking in. We've got the dogs coming and we'll flush Riley out in minutes," the Captain was taking in everything.

"Thanks Captain," I said.

Eli was on the stretcher. He looked at me and smiled, "You can't get rid of me this easy, Macy." Then they wheeled him through a barricade of officers to the ambulance.

I locked the front door and went to check the backdoor.

"I knew he was sweet on you. I hope you'll give him a chance, Macy," Sally Mae said knowingly.

I blushed to the roots of my hair. "Just start breakfast will you."

Sally Mae laughed as she headed to the kitchen. JJ handed me back the gun he had and headed to see if he could help Sally Mae. I paced from one end of the bunkhouse to the other. I was stuck inside while outside I could hear the dogs barking. I looked out the front window to see two officers flanking the door. I suspected there were two flanking the back door. I wanted to be out there hunting the man who shot Eli. I knew Eli would be okay, it's just I should have found a way to get word to him or at least gone back. Silly as it sounds, I was starting to like him. I found it to be strange, too. I thought I shut my heart to any kind of relationship and here I was wanting to know more about him. It was all this being cooped inside. I had too much restless energy. When my life got back to normal, I would get back in my routine.

"Macy, come eat. You're wearing a hole in the floor," JJ called.

I looked up to see him carrying plates to the table. Sally Mae followed with the coffee pot and the teapot she found somewhere. I went to the table. The food smelled wonderful.

"I never expected Riley to come back here," JJ said.

"Neither did I, JJ. I thought we were safe here," Sally Mae said.

"Well, that makes three of us. I really thought it was silly Eli had been assigned to be our guard. I am fully capable of keeping us safe," I insisted.

"You're a witness now. You have to be guarded. If you had your way, you'd be right out there making a target of yourself," he said.

"It would be one way to get to know Eli better, JJ. She could request a room near his in the hospital. She's not thinking straight," Sally Mae giggled.

I shook my head and dived into the scrambled eggs, bacon, and toast. Suddenly I was ravenous. Sally Mae and JJ watched as I ate as though I had not eaten in days. When breakfast was over, I cleaned up. It gave me something to do besides pacing.

The woods and farm had been swarming with cops for over two hours. My cell phone chirped. It was Tom.

"How are you holding up, Macy?" he asked.

"Well, JJ thinks he's going to have to replace flooring from my pacing. Otherwise I guess I'm okay, just worried about Ida and Eli," I assured him.

"I can help you with that. Ida is on an antibiotic and is resting well. Eli is going to be kept overnight and then released. You should be able to pick him up in the morning."

"How *am* I going to pick him up?" I asked sarcastically. "My car is at home in my garage."

He chuckled, "Well, I gave him your number, so he could call you. I suspect they won't give up until they catch Riley and he'll be taken in chains or a body bag."

Just then there were gunshots. I heard several. One of the dogs yelped.

"I've got to let you go, Tom. There's gunfire." I flipped the phone shut not giving him a chance to answer. I hauled JJ and Sally Mae down near the sofa so they were protected in case bullets came through the windows. The gunfire was closer than I liked. I felt bad for the officers guarding the doors; there was no shelter for them, nothing to hide behind; they were sitting ducks. Now was the time to wait. I hated waiting. I hated not being in the loop and knowing what was going on. Time crawled. There were no other gunshots.

My phone chirped and I jumped. I quickly flipped it open, "McVannel."

"Were you hoping they had me? They don't. You and your friends are sitting ducks. I'm coming to finish you off," Riley cackled into my phone then it went dead. I quickly dialed the captain.

"Wellington," he snapped.

"Captain, Riley just called me. He says we're sitting ducks and if he takes out the guards we will be."

"I'm on it," he said.

I shut off the phone. Sally Mae and JJ were just looking at me. Finally, JJ asked, "What do we do now?"

"You two get in the safe room. Crawl down the hallway so you don't create a shadow for someone to shoot at. Sally Mae, remember what I said about shooting first."

She nodded then followed JJ down the hallway. She stopped once to look back and I motioned her to keep going.

I heard the radios crackle outside the front door. I suspected the Captain was issuing orders. Hopefully they could find some cover. I didn't want anyone hurt on my account. Eli was already down no one else had to be. The next thing I heard was a car. Someone had pulled a car up out front. I heard scraping on the back porch. Then I remembered there had been a picnic table out there. Those guards were going to use it for whatever cover they could. It's why someone had pulled a car out front. I breathed easier knowing they were no longer out in the open.

I turned the kitchen table on its side. It would give some cover in the rear when the gunfire started. I also pushed the sofa cushions up. Making extra for the bullets to go through. I felt pretty secure where I was. Again, it was time to wait. It seemed like the day would go on forever. There was sound from the back. Had Riley found a way to sneak up on those officers?

No gunfire. It could be good and it could be bad.

Suddenly, I heard a sound I hadn't heard before. It was the sound of a helicopter. I didn't think the captain would have called for one in this area. I turned on the news station and put the volume on low. Sure enough, we had a news helicopter flying around outside. This was going to make apprehending Riley more difficult. The news report said police had him pinned down in the wooded area on the west side of the Appleton farm. You could see officers working in a grid through the woods. Two dogs were out front. I could see the officers barricaded outside the bunkhouse. I was watching for movement which was different or out of sync with the officers in the grid. It made me feel like I was helping. Time stretched and the afternoon shadows started making the hunt harder to see. They had to catch him before nightfall or all chance of finding him would be gone.

It's when I saw him. He was moving through the trees from limb to limb and tree to tree. He was heading for the house. He was going to try to jump to the roof. I picked up my phone to call the captain.

"Wellington," he said.

"Captain, he's in the trees. He's heading for the house. He's trying to make the roof of the bunkhouse. He'll be able to take the guards out from above."

"Got it, Macy. Lay low," he ordered.

I flipped the phone shut. Where did the chimney come into the house? There was no fireplace. Would the chimney be wide enough for a man? I didn't think one of Riley's size would fit. He was going to cut down the outside guards and try to break in the door.

Again, I heard the radios outside then the men talking. I knew they were trying to come up with a way to stop what Riley had in mind. I went back to watching the TV. I lost Riley while talking to the captain. It took me a minute to find him again. He was still making his way toward the bunkhouse. He had about three more trees to clear. Most of the police officers were still working the grid. *What is the captain doing?* I was glued to the TV screen, but my senses were on alert to movement outside the house. *Why weren't they all converging on the house?* It was then I understood what the captain was doing. He kept the men working in the grid so when Riley looked back he would think he outsmarted them. I could see at least two sharpshooters had moved to the north of Riley's location. They were going to take him out when he tried to get to the roof. I could only hope it would work.

Riley was going to be even more deadly if he got close to the bunkhouse. He wanted JJ *and* me dead. He was taking no prisoners and Sally Mae would end up being a victim, too. This was going to be his last stand. He would take me out first, because I was here. He would have to find JJ and Sally Mae. If they stayed put, they were be safe. I knew if I didn't holler down the stairs the coast was clear, Sally Mae would shoot the first person down the steps. There was no question. JJ was the wild card. If he heard a struggle up here, would he break cover and try to save me? If he did, it would be all over. I had to trust Sally Mae would be able to contain him.

I brought my mind back to the TV. He had one more tree. Was he going to make the roof? I could feel myself tense. I was anticipating something but, I wasn't sure what. It was then I saw Riley attempt another jump. Mid-jump I heard the rifle shot outside and on the screen I saw him fall. I wondered if he was dead or just wounded. Would they get to him or would he find somewhere else to slink away? I continued to watch the screen. I could see the officers from the grid moving to the area where Riley had fallen. The radios crackled outside. The whole thing had a surreal feel to it. I was here and part of it, but I was watching it on TV. The tension in my body drained and all I felt was numbness.

My phone chirped. I flipped it open and responded automatically, "McVannel."

"Macy, it's Eli. Are you safe?" he asked anxiously.

"Eli?" I felt tears running down my cheeks.

"Macy, talk to me. I've been watching on the TV. Are you okay?" I could hear the concern in his voice.

"In the bunkhouse, JJ and Sally Mae are in the safe room. Eli?" My brain wasn't registering it was him.

"Yes, it's me. I'm fine. I'll be released tomorrow. Will you come and get me?" he asked.

"Yes, I'll come. I need to go." I flipped the phone shut before he could say anything else. I turned off the TV and was waiting for the captain to come. I needed to go home. I needed to see Ida. I needed to be out of here. *Where was the captain? Why weren't they coming? Did Riley escape again?* I heard sirens. *What did they need sirens for? Were other officers down?* My mind was beyond what was happening. I was tense and unable to take in the sounds around me. *Was it over?* I sensed someone in the room and turned gun pointed. There was a man standing in the kitchen. *Where had he come from?* I stood saying, "Police raise your hands slowly."

He turned raising his hands, "Macy, it's me JJ. Macy, put the gun down." He continued holding his hands above his head.

I kept my gun trained on him. I heard running outside. There was a banging on the door. I went to open it not lowering my gun.

"Don't move," I told the man in the kitchen. He'd be able to reach a knife if I let him put his hands down but he wasn't moving. I stepped aside still holding my gun on the man. The captain came through the door first.

"McVannel, put that gun down," he ordered.

I looked at the captain and then at the gun in my hand. I then looked at the man in the kitchen. *JJ, I pointed my gun at JJ.* I laid my gun on the coffee table and sank to my knees.

"Get a paramedic in here," the captain shouted, then turned and asked, "JJ, are you okay?"

"I'm fine. I need to let Sally Mae out of the safe room. You take care of Macy," he said making his way down the hall. He returned a few minutes later his arm around Sally Mae. By then the paramedics were checking me out. One said something about shock and I needed to go to the hospital. I attempted to protest.

Sally Mae piped up, "Get her a room near Eli Patterson."

They put me on a stretcher. All I wanted to do was sleep. I think they put something in my IV. I was groggy. I heard the captain saying something but I couldn't make it out. I stopped fighting and lay back on the stretcher.

CHAPTER TWENTY-SEVEN

I awoke feeling fuzzy, sensing I was not in my own bed, and not at the bunkhouse. Someone was holding my hand. Slowly I opened my eyes and the first face I saw was Eli's, his blue eyes lit as he smiled, his black hair fell over his brow.

"What are you doing here?" I asked still feeling groggy.

"Waiting for my sleeping beauty to awaken. Glad to have you back, Macy."

I felt myself blushing as I looked around and found myself in a hospital bed. It was coming back to me now. I lost it at the last minute and was going to be in trouble.

"JJ?" I started glancing around.

"He and Sally Mae are waiting outside. They've been here since early this morning," Eli told me.

"Ida, how is Ida?" I was still trying to fight off the fatigue which was clouding my brain.

"She's doing fine and should be released by tomorrow. Sally Mae is going to move in with her until she's back on her feet," he explained patiently.

"Thank goodness. I'm so glad. How are you?" I anxiously asked him.

"I'm fine and as soon as they release you we're going to go some place and get to know each other better," he promised.

"You think so?" I smiled.

"I know so. I have it on good authority you are *not* to return to your job for a week and I am not going back for two," he winked as if he knew a secret.

"So, where are we going for this week, while I recuperate?" I asked feeling like a giddy teen.

"Not so fast. I'm keeping our destination a secret," Eli teased.

"Which means you have to trust him, Macy," Sally Mae said.

I felt myself starting to blush as I looked up to see she and JJ had entered the room. "I'm glad to see you two are okay. JJ, I'm sorry for pointing my weapon at you," I apologized.

"It's forgotten, Macy. You were under a lot of pressure and sleep deprived," he said as if it hadn't happened.

"Thank you. Sally Mae, I hear you've found someone else to baby-sit," I said grinning.

"I'm going to love taking care of Ida and Mike's mom is going to be stopping in, too. As soon as we can get everything settled, we're moving JJ's mom to Rivers Edge," her bubbly enthusiasm was contagious.

"Sounds like everyone's got a plan. Has anyone seen or heard from Tom?" I wanted to know.

"He brought Shannon in a while ago. Her water broke, so they're just waiting for this one to arrive," Sally Mae informed us.

I gave Eli a stricken look. "We *can't* leave until the baby is born."

"Stop fretting, I know," he said as if calming a whining child.

The nurse came in and shooed everyone out. "I think you can safely get dressed. Your lady friend brought you some clean clothes. I'll get them out while you shower and dress."

I thanked her and headed for the shower. When I came out she had laid the clothing on the bed. I did a double-take when I noticed some of the garments weren't mine. The jeans looked familiar, but the lacy underwear—which I didn't even own--and the blouse weren't mine. Since I had no other choice, I put them on. I was brushing out my hair when they came back in.

Both JJ and Eli whistled. I looked at Sally Mae and she grinned from ear to ear.

"Well, you can't look good in sweats all the time," she teased.

I felt myself blushing again. The blouse a powder blue which clung to me like a slim-fitted t-shirt. She included a navy blue shrug style sweater to go over it. The outfit made me a bit exposed but she included my favorite musk rose perfume.

"We just got word Tom and Shannon have a baby girl. Shall we go welcome her?" Sally Mae asked excitedly.

I signed the papers the nurse had for me. Although we were both discharged, hospital policy dictated we would be in wheelchairs until we left the premises. JJ and Sally Mae offered to wheel us around.

Tom was in the nursery, with his daughter in his arms, when we arrived. When he saw us, he came forward and held her up to show her off. She was beautiful. He handed her back to the nurse and came to join us. "Let's go see Shannon." He led the way to her room where she lay on the bed looking tired, yet radiant.

"Macy, I hear you are being sprung today," though tired Shannon's voice sounded cheerful.

"Yes, but we had to see the baby first. She's beautiful," I gushed.

Tom had gone to stand beside his wife. While the nurses had supplied a small bottle of champagne for the couple, Tom had procured a larger one and had it chilling in ice. He quickly popped the cork and handed paper cups of wine all around. Eli declined saying it would mess up his antibiotic.

Tom lifted his cup to toast, "To my lovely wife and daughter."

"Here, here." We all said as we drank to their health.

"And now for the big announcement," Shannon said quietly. "We are naming her Macy Ida-Mae Maxwell."

"No, Shannon, you needn't name her after me," I protested.

"Nonsense, Macy, who else would I name her after? You are the person who makes sure my husband comes home to me each night. I know you always have his back."

I blushed and tears came to my eyes. I felt humbled.

"We've talked about it and we want you all to be her godparents. So, if anything should happen to us we know she'll be well cared for," Tom added.

"I don't think you mean me," Eli said.

"You're wrong," Tom answered looking meaningfully at me. "You took my place and the bullet could very well have been for me."

"I'm going to speak for Sally Mae and me and say we'd be honored," JJ responded as he reached to shake hands with Tom.

I looked at both Tom and Shannon feeling totally overwhelmed. "This is quite an honor, are you sure?"

"We've been talking about it for days. Please say you agree," Shannon's soft voice touched me.

We agreed. Then we said our good-byes.

On the way down to the car, I asked Sally Mae if she knew of a place I could get a bouquet of fresh flowers. Without answering she dashed off quickly—most likely to the gift shop.

JJ escorted us to the discharge area in our wheelchairs. I was surprised to see a limousine waiting for us. Sally Mae returned with a beautiful bouquet of colorful flowers perfectly arranged. The driver came around to open the back door and Eli helped me into the back. The door closed and we were whisked away. Sally Mae and JJ stood on the sidewalk waving.

"So, where are we going? I have reports to write and I need to know how Ida is," I told Eli.

"Watch this." He turned on a video on the TV screen.

Ida was sitting in her hospital room. She looked into the camera as she spoke, "Macy, you are a wonder. I have no recollection of you and the boys taking me to my house. I don't even remember the ambulance ride. I did hear Eli was hurt returning to the safety of the bunkhouse. I also hear he'll recover quickly. As for you get some rest this week. I'll be ready with iced tea when you return and you can tell me everything. Thank you for bringing me closure in Bobby James' death. Come see me soon."

I wiped my eyes as Ida faded from the screen revealing the captain. "McVannel, I need you back here in a week ready to go. Since I know you won't rest until you know everything, I'm going to brief you now. Riley was only wounded by our sniper but, suffered a couple of broken bones. Which was our plan, because we wanted him to stand trial. He's in a maximum hospital facility in solitary confinement and only gets to see his attorney, doctors, and nurses. He's been arraigned on three counts of murder, two counts of attempted murder, theft, and several accounts of criminal trespass. He won't go back into court before you get home. This case was a pressure cooker; you take the next week, then come home and finish your reports. We'll have lots of work waiting for you. With you and Maxwell out of my hair for awhile, I might even start to like this job again." He was laughing as the video faded out to mark the end.

"Eli, can we make a quick stop?"

He looked at the flowers Sally Mae had handed me, "Just tell me where."

Five minutes later, we rolled up to Maple Valley Cemetery. I got out and walked through the tombstones to the one I was looking for. It read:

Craig Wiles
Died in the Line of Duty.

I laid the flowers at the base and spoke softly as I said my final good-bye. I knew he would want me to move on and would approve of Eli. I said good-bye one last time and walked to the limo. Once inside the car rolled away. I still didn't know where I was going, but I knew I was going to enjoy the ride. I took the glass of wine Eli offered me and settled back into the seat. I closed my eyes and let go of the regrets I had. It was time to start living again.

ACKNOWLEDGMENTS

I cannot thank my editors enough. They read my writing and find my mistakes. I am blessed to have three editors for this book. My mom, Donavee Vigus, who tells me she's read part of this already. My daughter, Jamie Kline, who uses her fine toothed comb when she edits. She fits editing in between working full-time, going to college part-time, and running between sporting events for her two amazing children. This book I had a special editor, Lori Janczewski, who works more jobs than I can count, and was my right hand at work for years. I cannot thank you enough for all you have done.

Special thanks go to the ladies of the Fictionista Writers Collective who put me in touch with two wonderful and talented writers, Cesya MaRae Cuono and Sherrice Thomas whose insights made this a much better novel than it started out to be. I love you both.

I am also going to thank my many readers and fans. You keep pushing me to write more and better novels. I will keep writing as long as you keep reading.

ABOUT THE AUTHOR

Retired teacher Rebecka Vigus spends her time writing, reading, crocheting, hiking, and swimming. She travels seeking the ideal place to call home. Ms. Vigus has been writing since she was in her pre-teens. Her first book was poetry, *Only a Start and Beyond*. Since then she has penned five, full-length novels, one book for children, several short stories, and even a self-help book for tweens and teens. Ms. Vigus has been listed as a Michigan Author and Illustrator at the State of Michigan website.

9 781946 848758